Dead Still

"Lean closer, if you will, suh. Put both hands on the desk top so you can study it."

Lassiter leaned down and shook his head. "As I said, I'm in no mood for games."

"This is no game," Ormsby snapped. "This is a drawing of a special weapon. Made for me by a craftsman."

Lassiter felt a chill of apprehension. He didn't move a muscle but stood hunched over the desk top. "Go on," he said, "tell me the rest of it."

"That weapon is under mah desk. A revolver in a special frame. With a hair trigger. All ah have to do is touch it with mah foot. If ah do, you are dead. So do not move. Do not even twitch."

Other *Leisure* books by Jack Slade:

Lassiter: Brother Gun

LASSITER:
Redgate Gold

JACK SLADE

LEISURE BOOKS  NEW YORK CITY

A LEISURE BOOK®

February 2010

Published by

Dorchester Publishing Co., Inc.
200 Madison Avenue
New York, NY 10016

ISBN 10: 0-8439-6370-0
ISBN 13: 978-0-8439-6370-0
E-ISBN: 978-1-4285-0814-9

Printed in the United States of America.

10 9 8 7 6 5 4 3 2 1

LASSITER:
Redgate Gold

Chapter One

When the two strangers slogged aboard the westbound, rainwater spilling from hatbrims and slickers, Lassiter recognized trouble. He was dead for sleep and to minimize risk had tied the heavy brown satchel to his ankle with a length of rawhide. Just in case some thief had ideas about making off with a bag that contained nearly twenty thousand dollars in gold coins.

Until they reached the flag stop at Delon, there had been only one other passenger, a fat drummer at the front of the coach. Sample cases were piled in the adjoining seat. He alternately snored or played checkers with the conductor. Hardly the type to try and rob a man while he slept, but Lassiter took no chances.

And now as the train *chuff-chuffed* its way out of the flag stop, Lassiter knew sleep was out of the question. The two obvious hardcases with their beard stubble and grimy clothes were the same as those he'd been meeting for nearly a month since taking on the job of moving Ormsby cattle east to Sahuaro Junction.

Before taking the job, Lassiter had been down to his last peso after a misadventure in Chihuahua diamonds that involved a pretty young widow. He had barely made made the border ahead of a swarm of rurales spurred on by a powerful politico.

Lassiter had ridden north on a spent horse, looking for something that would pull him out of the financial quagmire. He mentioned it to a bartender. Lassiter was overheard by a slicker who foolishly sought to sell him a "genuine" map of the Redgate millions. Lassiter was in no mood for foolishness. He'd seen such maps before, properly weathered and with ink fading. They were for greenhorns or other empty-headed fortune seekers. It hurt Lassiter's pride that he'd been taken for one. When the would-be map seller persisted and became belligerent, he and a companion ended up on the cantina floor.

Lassiter's outburst had been witnessed by Leland Ormsby. Despite advanced years, Ormsby retained a Machiavellian mind and an abiding interest in young females. He was a frail husk of a man in a whipcord suit. He asked Lassiter to join him at a comer table.

"I'm an old man and I don't have long," Ormsby explained over drinks at the scene of Lassiter's eruption. His voice held a trace of the deep South. Ormsby had already paid for the two chairs the hapless victims had smashed in their backward flight off Lassiter's fists. "I'm selling off every head of cattle on my ranch," Ormsby said. "You want a job as my foreman?"

Lassiter knew of the sprawling Ormsby ranch with its private lake. Lassiter didn't wonder about a rancher selling off all his cows, he didn't even haggle over salary. He wanted time to let down, to have three squares, a dry bed, whiskey, a woman and a chance to forget the firing squad that came close to splattering him all over an adobe wall in Chihuahua.

"I want to get rid of my present foreman," Ormsby said, speaking precisely as if trying to rid himself of the Southem accent. "Have you got guts enough to fire him?"

"Show him to me."

Ormsby gave his old man's dry cackle. "He's outside."

"Let's go."

Joe Tarsh was a big scowling man, two inches or so over Lassiter's five-eleven, with heavy shoulders. Lassiter's hair and brows were dark, his smile sardonic. Tarsh had wavy yellow hair, long lashes and a protruding lower lip partially hidden by a downsweep of pale mustache.

Tarsh was helping a slim dark-haired young woman put some bundles in the bed of a spring wagon. When she saw Lassiter emerge from the cantina, her pretty mouth fell open in surprise. Ormsby was hobbling along at Lassiter's side, a fox-in-the-chicken-house grin on his lips.

Tarsh looked around to see what had caught the young woman's attention. He saw Ormsby. "Hiya, boss." Then his hard blue gaze swung to Lassiter.

Ormsby nudged Lassiter. "Tell him."

"Ormsby just hired me. I'm foreman."

Tarsh squinted at Lassiter in his dusty clothes, a two-day stubble on strong jaws. "I'm foreman," Tarsh said, and squared his shoulders.

"You're fired," Lassiter armounced calmly.

"Who the hell said so!" Tarsh shouted, his face beginning to redden.

"I did," Lassiter replied. "From here on out, I hire and I fire."

Ormsby clapped skeletal hands together. "Bravo, bravo!"

Tarsh shouted, swore, made a move toward his gun. But he was too late. Lassiter's .44 was aimed at the man's belly.

Those in the cantina came outside to watch Lassiter disarm Tarsh. Ruiz, the cantina owner, spoke to Lassiter. "How easy you make enemies." He laughed and pointed at one of the map sellers who had a broken jaw. The other suffered a smashed nose. Then Ruiz jerked his head at Tarsh who was riding away, shoulders stiff with anger. "Three enemies you made."

"A habit I've got," Lassiter grunted.

Ormsby drove the spring wagon to the ranch, the pretty dark-haired young woman sharing the seat. Her name was Claire. Whenever the road was wide enough so Lassiter would swing alongside the wagon, he sensed her studying him from the corners of her eyes. He had a feeling she thought she knew him. But so far as he was concerned she was a stranger.

At the ranch Ormsby took Lassiter to his office. A herd had already been gathered, according to Ormsby. Lassiter's first job was to take the herd to Sahuaro Junction where a cattle buyer would be waiting.

"I want payment in gold," Ormsby instructed him. "Gold has always been my luck."

"That kind of luck I like." Lassiter gave Ormsby a hard grin. He had to admire the old man who despite advanced years had acquired a mistress in Claire.

"Some men might say I'm a fool to trust you to bring that money back to me." Ormsby was seated behind a flat-topped desk, dwarfed in an oversize padded leather chair. "Am I a fool, Lassiter?"

"No." In other matters such as Ormsby stripping his own range of every cow, there might be room for doubt.

"You will return with the money?" Ormsby's bright eyes probed Lassiter's weary face.

"If I give my word, I'll be back."

"Your word, then."

Lassiter gave his word.

The dark-haired Claire entered the office. She had changed into a clinging green dress that matched the color of her eyes. A string of pearls encircled a pale neck. In some ways she reminded Lassiter of Dona Esperanza, the sultry widow of Chihuahua.

"You've met Claire Manning," Ormsby said, gesturing at the woman in the doorway. "By the way, I am a very jealous man."

"So am I, when I have something I like." Lassiter smiled at her. She barely nodded her head.

"I didn't realize you were talking business, Leland," she said, and left the office.

Later that evening Lassiter was smoking a cigar in a tipped-back chair in front of his new quarters. In two days he was to hire a crew to replace the one Tarsh had ramrodded, and start moving the herd east to the railroad.

Claire Manning approached. "You don't remember me, do you, Lassiter?" she said softly.

He stood up. "I'd like to say I do. But why lie? If I was ever with you, I must have been drunk not to remember."

"We weren't ever . . . together. You got out of town too soon. I was dancing at a place in Santa Fe. I remember the night you beat two card sharks out of sixty thousand dollars."

Lassiter shrugged at the memory. "I could use some of it now."

"You're down on your luck. So was I. Till I met Leland." She looked over her shoulder at the big house. Lamplighted windows glowed through cottonwoods. Beyond the house the manmade lake shimmered in the moonlight.

She hesitated, toyed with the ends of a mantilla draped over her shoulders to ward off the chill of the desert evening. "You heard Leland speak of jealousy. He thought Tarsh and me . . ." She looked down at the ground. Lassiter smiled at her attempt to be embarrassed.

"I kind of figured it that way," he said.

"I was afraid of Tarsh. Thank God he's gone and you're here."

"I'm beginning to like the idea myself."

"I'll come right to the point. I want to have a talk with you . . . later."

"Ormsby a light sleeper?" he drawled.

"Once Leland's through with me for the night he sleeps like it's the end of everything. Sometimes when I go in in the morning and try to wake him up, I think he's dead." She hugged her arms. "God, it's an eerie feeling."

"I can imagine."

She stepped closer so that he caught her scent. His backbone began to glow. He'd had a good meal in the bunkhouse and a couple of drinks. But no woman. Not yet.

Claire said softly, "I know about money. Enough for both of us for the rest of our lives."

"Tell me about it."

"You're the partner I've been praying for. I was afraid to trust Joe Tarsh. He'd cut my throat and take everything for himself. I know his kind."

He wondered how much he could believe. "Money interests me," he said.

"In two hours I'll meet you at the far side of the lake."

When they did meet, she only hinted at the money. Lassiter didn't press her. With Tarsh, she had been fearful of romance and held herself back. So she claimed. With Lassiter she was more than willing. For the first time since the debacle in Chihuahua he almost forgot the pretty widow of his late friend, Don Benito.

Even after he and Claire were walking back toward the shadowed house, arm in arm, skirting the lake, she only gave him a few tantalizing hints about the money mentioned earlier.

"Come back to me, Lassiter, from the cattle sale. Then I'll tell you. Between the two of us we'll be rich . . . rich!"

"I'll be back. I gave Ormsby my word."

Her green eyes sparkled in moonlight under the cottonwoods. "It's a promise of wealth that will bring you back to me."

"You alone are enough of a lure. Hell, after I've sampled paradise you think I'd refuse second helpings?" It didn't hurt to flatter her.

"Paradise," she scoffed. But he knew she was pleased.

In parting she said, "Think of the money you'll collect for the cattle. Multiply it by ten, by a hundred, by a thousand—by ten thousand!"

He couldn't help but be caught up in her excitement. "I'll be back."

"While you're on the trail, keep your eyes open for Tarsh," she warned. "And he's got friends."

At Sahuaro Junction he collected money from the cattle buyer, then got suspicious of the pickup crew he had hired after overhearing two of them mutter a name to the others: "Tarsh."

He paid them off, told them to stay the hell away from him. Two of them argued. They tried to jump him. One of them he flatted with a gun barrel and the other with a boot toe in the groin. The other three backed off.

And now he was on his way back in a jolting railroad coach. At least the westbound passenger coach, hooked onto a string of empty box cars, was better than the cattle train he'd ridden east to the junction.

When the two hardcases came dripping aboard at the flagstop at Delon, Lassiter smelled more trouble. They plopped into the seat across from him. The big one with broad cheekbones and black beard stubble weighed over two hundred and fifty pounds. He introduced himself as Tiny Corum. His companion was Petey. Lassiter didn't get the last name. He didn't care. They were staring at the satchel tied to Lassiter's ankle.

In clipped tones Lassiter suggested the men move forward in the car a few seats. "If I have to keep an eye on you sitting across from me I'll get a crick in my neck."

"We set where we want," Corum blustered. His shorter companion, Petey, nudged Corum and gestured at the snout of the revolver Lassiter had slid across the seat arm.

Lassiter's dark eyes were cold. "Tell Tarsh he wasted his time hiring you two."

Corum's jaw dropped. "Tarsh? Never heard of no Tarsh."

Lassiter gestured with the cocked .44. The pair slouched on up the aisle, wet slickers bunched under their arms. Each man wore a holstered revolver.

Rain lashed the windows, pelted the roof. The conductor finished his checkers game with the fat drummer at the front of the car. He came down the swaying coach to collect fares from the new passengers. "Looks like you fellas got caught in the cloudburst," he observed, sucking on false teeth. "Second one we had in a week. How far you goin'?"

Corum named the next stop, Andover. The conductor charged them a dollar each. They paid reluctantly. They might be broke now, but close at hand were riches. Their luck had changed abruptly that morning two miles out of Delon. A flash flood swept away the horses they had stolen the previous afternoon. Another traveler ahead of them suffered a similar misfortune. This one lost a loaded pack mule and a fine-looking gray horse. He was an older man wearing a beaver hat and a worn plum-colored suit.

"What a terrible flood," the stranger gasped when Tiny Corum and Petey walked up. Corum shoved a .45 in the man's startled face. "What you got in your pockets? Search him, Petey."

Petey found eight silver dollars. They suspected he had money hidden on him because the loaded pack mule and the roan lost in the flood had meant a sizeable investment. The man was on his knees, pleading.

Petey found a folded paper hidden under the man's shirt. It was weathered and had been folded and refolded so many times that the creases were deep. Corum was illiterate, but Petey could read, after a fashion. Petey's lips moved as he laboriously made out words in the faded text.

"Where I buried my gold," Petey read. "Signed, Colonel Redgate." It was dated April 16, 1865. There was the name of a settlement, Andover, on the map. Also on the map was a large X in the center of a stretch of country known as "The Furnace."

"We'll be rich, by God!" Corum cried and shot the stranger in the head. It was only another dead man to them. After breaking out of a Missouri jail they had murdered and shot their way west.

The same cloudburst that had generated the flash flood struck them when they were within sight of a flag stop known as Delon. They were in good spirits despite the deluge when a train hooted in the distance. After paying their fare it left them six of the dead stranger's silver dollars. If they were going to hunt for buried gold they'd need a stake. That was why the brown leather satchel tied to the ankle of the lean dark stranger in the first seat had attracted their attention.

Corum spoke quietly up to the conductor who was punching their two tickets. "What's so precious in that bag he's got tied to his boot?"

The conductor, holding a seat edge to maintain balance in the rocking coach, did not even look back. "Wouldn't mess with him," he advised. "That's Lassiter."

Petey thought it was funny. "Messin' with people is what we do best."

Corum said, "Who's Tarsh, anyhow?"

"Never heard of him," the conductor said.

The conductor swayed to the front of the coach and took his seat across from the fat man and his sample cases.

"Who got on at Delon?" the drummer wanted to know.

"Couple drifters, looks like. Got their eye on that bag of Lassiter's."

"What you reckon's in that bag, anyhow?"

"Knowin' Lassiter's rep, it might be diamonds." The conductor had heard rumors of Lassiter's troubles in Chihuahua. He gave a dry laugh, adjusted his store teeth and settled down to another game of checkers.

Tiny Corum eyed the two men bent over the checker-board. When the train slowed for Andover, he and Petey would make their move. If necessary, they'd kill the two up front as well as the dark stranger with the satchel. Then he and Petey would jump off the slowing train with the satchel and cross over into Mexico. On the map it looked about a hundred yards. At full dark they'd sneak back and start hunting for gold. They were familiar with the Redgate story. There was said to be a million dollars buried somewhere. And they had a map.

"Get ready," Corum said under his breath.

Chapter Two

Lassiter was half asleep, thinking of the homecoming with Claire. Only a few more hours and he'd report to Leland Ormsby. Then after the old man fell asleep for the night, he and Claire would adjourn to the far side of the private lake. Just thinking of her long and lively legs crossed at his backbone was enough to warm the blood. The voices of the newcomers reached him from the middle of the car.

Petey was laughing. "After we dig up the money we kin live like kings over in Old May-heeco."

"Shut up," his big companion warned.

Lassiter shed his dreams of Claire. The pair up front had the rattlesnake look of men who lived by the gun. He untied the bag from his ankle. To be ready, just in case.

As he settled back in the seat, he thought of the border within sprinting distance of Andover. He thought about it as the train rattled and jolted its way over the roadbed that was even in worse shape than it had been the last time he had ridden this line. Wouldn't have been the first time he ran for the border with his pockets crammed with Yankee dollars. But there was only twenty thousand in the satchel. He needed eighty thousand more. It might take a hundred thousand dollars to buy back the rancho that had belonged to Don Benito. His widow deserved it. Don Benito had once saved Lassiter from *ley fuga*. Had it not been for Lassiter's good friend,

Mexico carbines would have blown him to pieces. That was some years ago.

Lassiter set the satchel on the seat beside him. It had considerable weight and gave off a faint clinking sound of the gold coins Ormsby had insisted on.

Corum happened to look back at that moment, saw the bag, and noted that it was heavy. He seemed pleased.

Grin, you bastard, Lassiter thought. He was jumpy. Hell, he'd been under a strain since leaving the Ormsby OS ranch with the cattle, wondering which of the pickup crew would try and kill him while he slept. He hadn't trusted a one of them. But it had been the only crew he could line up on such short notice. He wondered how Claire and Ormsby and the formidable Mexican cook, Mercedes, had fared with the men he had left at the ranch as guards. He'd soon know.

A buildup of ominous clouds over distant mountains caught his eye. Lassiter swore under his breath. Another cloudburst might catch him riding an unfamiliar horse across the Furnace. Andover was only a few miles ahead. And just then he felt the coach give a sudden lurch. There was a grinding of couplings. Something crashed up ahead. The coach swayed violently, throwing him out of the seat. He landed hard on his knees. There was a great thumping of iron wheels on wooden ties. He grabbed the satchel and tried to reach his feet. Just as he clutched the heavy satchel against his stomach, the coach went over. He crashed to the roof of the car as it landed upside down. The weighted satchel slammed him on the head. Windows exploded into a hailstorm of glass particles. With a clang of metal and splintering wood, the coach toppled against a cutbank.

Tiny Corum was yelling. "The satchel! Let's get him, Petey!"

In the sudden stillness, Corum, on the roof of the car that was now the floor, looked around for his friend. Petey wasn't going to help him get anyone, ever. Petey was pinned against a seat above. A three-inch strip of siding from the splintered coach wall had caught him dead center through the chest. There was a look of surprise on his face. Corum turned his back on Petey who dangled in the air like a speared fish. He crawled along the buckled roof of the upended car. When he was within a few feet of Lassiter, he started to reach for a gun.

Lassiter sat up in the welter of glass and splintered wood just as Corum's weapon cleared leather. Lassiter's .44, half-hidden by the satchel, spat a pencil of flame. As it roared, Corum looked as surprised as his dead friend Petey. He fell face down onto some broken glass. Lassiter doubted if he felt any of it. Lassiter removed his black hat and gingerly felt his skull where the satchel had struck him. But there was no blood. That much luck, anyhow. That he was still alive was the real luck.

At the front of the coach the fat drummer was flat on his back on the crumpled roof, mouth open. Nearby was the conductor. A set of dentures gleamed white as a salt bar in the wreckage.

As Lassiter picked up the money satchel, the conductor sat up and reached for his teeth. At the same moment the fat man came to his knees to stare numbly at the twisted metal. Two seats had been torn loose and were dangling overhead by single bolts.

Lassiter climbed to his feet. "Let's clear out of here!" The conductor stared questioningly at the two unshaven passengers.

"Dead," Lassiter offered.

"Swore I heard a gunshot," wheezed the fat drummer.

"So much noise everything sounded like gunshots," Lassiter said and climbed through a shattered window. Let the law think both strangers had been killed in the wreck. He'd worry later if a bullet hole was found in the big one. At the moment he wanted no more delays in explaining it to a sheriff.

Lassiter dropped to the ground, saw that the locomotive had been derailed but remained upright when tracks had been washed out by the cloudburst earlier in the day. Most of the empty box cars were splintered. Behind the coach the caboose lay on its side.

"Jesus, I figured I was a goner sure," panted the fat man as he emerged from the wreckage.

The conductor clambered through a broken window, waving a square of yellowed paper. "Looky what one of them dead ones had in his shirt pocket. Another one of them there Colonel Redgate treasure maps. Ain't seen one in a spell."

"I have," Lassiter grunted.

"The old Mex across the line must be back in the mapmaking business," the conductor said with a shake of the head. "It's usually a tenderfoot buys them maps. Them two dead hardcases didn't seem the kind."

A white-faced brakeman was just climbing out of the caboose. He jerked a thumb at the overturned coach. "Everybody all right?"

"Two dead," announced the conductor gravely.

"Thought I heard a gun go off," said the brakeman.

Lassiter stood holding the heavy satchel. He asked the brakeman how far it was to Andover.

The man squinted toward the west. "Three mile, reckon. You figure to walk, I'll go along. Got to hit the telegraph shack an' git a wreckin' crew out here."

"Hey, Ben," sang out the conductor as the brakeman and Lassiter walked away, "sell you a Redgate map cheap!"

The brakeman waved back to the grinning conductor to indicate he could appreciate a good joke. While the brakeman paused to make sure the engineer and fireman were uninjured, Lassiter lengthened his stride. He didn't want company. The brakeman never did catch up to him.

Joe Tarsh finished his drink in Andover's only saloon and with his two companions climbed the outside stairway to the second floor of the Grand Palace Hotel. It was a tall, narrow wooden building that fronted the gleaming railroad tracks and Mexico, a hundred yards or so away. At one time there had been a town over there but *insurrectos* in one of the periodic uprisings against Porfirio Diaz, had burned it. The town had never been rebuilt on the Mexican side of the line.

"Train's due in a few minutes," Tarsh said, hurrying his climb up the stairs. Sweat matted his thick pale mustache.

"Can't figure out how you know he'll be on that damn train," Eddie Danno grumbled. He was chunky, redhaired and with a scar across the bridge of his nose.

Tarsh chuckled. "I keep my ear to the ground, that's how I know."

"But in Tres Vidas the word is that he's comin' back through San Pablo. That's up nawth."

Tarsh didn't reply to that. "If he ain't on this train, he'll be on the next one."

The third man was thin and short of breath. "Jesus, these damn stairs get steeper every time." J. D.

Tramble was bunched and asthmatic. "I don't want to wait ova for another train."

"Cheer up, J. D.," Tarsh called down to him. "Plenty of whiskey in town an' we've got Ruby."

Tarsh was at the landing. He tried the door and a girl's voice said, "Busy!"

"Well, hurry it up, Ruby," Tarsh called through the door. "Mornin' train's about due."

There were sudden frantic sounds of motion coming from the hotel room. Then in a few moments the door opened. A little man came out, ducking his head in embarrassment. He carried a coat over his arm and was tucking in his shirttail. Tarsh and the others stood aside to let him down the narrow stairs.

Tarsh grinned at the man's embarrassment, then entered the room. A slender blond girl was just putting on a wrapper. "Leave it off, Ruby," Tarsh said.

"But you said I was to stand in the window."

"Yeah."

"Gosh, I just can't stand there . . . you know, with nothin' on."

Tarsh gave in to a point. "Leave it unbuttoned. But show a lot. Understand?" He walked over and slung an arm around her slender waist. "You're a good-lookin' gal, Ruby, an' it's a shame to keep so much of you hid."

J. D. Tramble leaned against the door frame, out of breath. "How the hell you know Ruby standin' there is gonna fetch Lassiter upstairs?"

"Found out a few things about that hombre," Tarsh said with a wink. "He's got one weakness. Purty gals. An' our Ruby here fits that bill. Ain't that right, Ruby?"

"You always do say nice things to me, Joe," she said, sitting on the edge of the bed. "You're not going to kill him in here, are you?"

"If he gets tough, we might throw him out the window is all." Tarsh laughed and chucked Ruby under the chin. "Don't look so worried. All we want is his money. Two hundred of it is yours. Like I promised." Tarsh had no intention of killing Lassiter unless it came to saving his own life. There was a price on Lassiter's head in Chihuahua. Tarsh considered it would be a bonus for all the hell Lassiter had caused him with Ormsby.

While they waited for the train, Ruby thought of what two hundred dollars in one lump sum would mean. She could buy some decent clothes and go north to Denver and see her sister again. She wiped at her eyes.

Eddie Danno dragged a gold watch from his pocket. He had stolen it at San Luis. "Hell, train's way past due. What the hell you figure happened?"

"Just simmer down, Eddie. It'll be along." But Tarsh began to fret himself. To pass the time, they went over the plan again. "You get Lassiter real interested, Ruby.

Don't talk money. That's a waste of time. Just act like you can't wait to make him happy. Then when he's so happy he's ready to yell, we come outa the closet."

"Don't forget Lassiter's one tough sonofabitch," Tramble reminded. "It ain't gonna be like pickin' strawberries."

"Two fellas are walkin' along the tracks," said Danno from the window. "One of 'em is carryin' a bag."

Tarsh sprang to the window. "Lassiter!"

Chapter Three

Andover squatted at the edge of the desert, a collection of mud and frame structures that in the distance reminded Lassiter of warts on a hog's back. Twenty yards behind him the brakeman was plodding along, sweating in the heat.

The first building in town was a cantina. There Lassiter paused to burn out frustration and tiredness with a double shot of whiskey. He sized up the four other patrons: vaqueros from across the line. They didn't seem threatening. He still wasn't sure but what the dead pair in the wreckage hadn't been hired by Joe Tarsh to steal the cattle money and kill him. Splitting the money later with Tarsh. He didn't expect to see Tarsh here in Andover, but he was taking no chances. He had told everyone that he intended returning from the cattle sale on another rail line, getting a horse at San Pablo and riding south to the Ormsby ranch.

Picking up the satchel, he stepped out into the bright morning. He stood a moment to adjust his eyes to the sun glare. There was't much to the town, just the cantina, a hotel, a few shacks spread out among sand dunes and cactus and a livery stable. As he stood there he was aware of a persistent coldness at the nape of his neck. Nobody knew he was coming home via Andover except old man Ormsby. And Claire. So why did he have that hunch that there might be trouble?

Lassiter stared in the direction of Mexico, only a few yards to the south. With the contents of the brown satchel he could live like a *rico*. At least be rich for a time. But there was Don Benito's widow, Esperanza, to consider. Only eighty thousand dollars more. Claire had mentioned money. Big money.

He owed Don Benito's memory. While Don Benito lived, Lassiter had never even considered invading the bed of the pretty and much younger wife. But Don Benito unfortunately had finally misjudged the political climate of Chihuahua a year ago and was framed for a crime and finished off in what was known as *ley fuga*, "law of flight." What Lassiter himself had once faced. They give you a chance to run for it, sometimes the soldiers making bets as to how far you'd be able to run before the legs were shot out from under and the job finished with a slug through the brain.

He started walking toward the livery barn which was beyond the hotel, the heavy bag swinging from a long arm.

He noticed a girl come to a window on the hotel's second floor, leaning out. She wore a pink wrapper that hung open. She had good breasts.

"Come upstairs, handsome!" she called to him. She had a nice smile, but he detected nervousness. And even embarrassment as she folded the wrapper around her. He noticed that her hands trembled and there was a beading of sweat on her forehead. She was either new to the business or somebody was standing behind her with a gun. Too many years he'd spent along the border to press his luck.

He called up to her. "Be with you soon's I see about getting myself a horse. Five minutes and I'll be up."

He waved to her and she waved back. And just before he slipped around a corner of the building, he looked back. He saw her saying something over her shoulder to someone in the room.

In an alley he hurriedly counted out a hundred dollars from the satchel. He strapped up the satchel again and hurried on to the livery barn.

"I want a saddle and a horse," he said to a gaunt, toothless man.

"Ain't got nothin' cheap," the stableman said wisely.

Lassiter had told the girl he'd be back in five minutes. It was a little less than ten when he rode out of the livery barn astride the best horse the man had for sale, and setting a warped saddle. The man had thrown in lashings and a tarp. The bag was wrapped in the tarp which was tied on behind the cantle. He got out of Andover in a hurry. The girl in the window would grow wrinkled waiting for him.

He urged the bony gray horse to a faster pace because of the buildup of a storm that he hoped to beat. He also hoped the damned horse lasted long enough to get him back to the Ormsby ranch.

The same bank of clouds he had noticed from the train still hovered like a black mantle over distant mountains. A cloudburst rarely killed anyone unless he was fool enough to ride into a canyon and get caught in a flash flood. A sandstorm was another thing; the Furnace was noted for them. It could simply swallow you up. He thought it was too early in the year for them, but such things were tricky to predict.

It was a stretch of desert that an early traveler, half dead from heat and thirst, had dubbed the Furnace. Many wild tales were told about that bit of frontier he was about to cross, known locally as "the twenty nines of hell." One story had it that there was a lost cavalry patrol presumably buried under sand dunes that literally moved under the lash of treacherous winds. There was also supposed to be an Indian horse-raiding party that had simply vanished during one of the storms.

And there was no accounting for the many who were believed to have perished while searching for buried treasure. The two dead hardcases back in the smashed railroad coach with their map of Redgate millions could have become current victims. Thinking about the Redgate map caused Lassiter to explode with laughter. It made the bony horse skittish. Lassiter swore and pulled it in.

"I even think about Colonel Redgate," Lassiter muttered, "and this fool horse tries to dump me on my head."

Lassiter laughed again, more softly this time. Days of tension and lack of sleep had dulled his mind.

From time to time he glanced over his shoulder, but there was no sign of anyone coming in his direction out of Andover. Could he have been wrong about the girl in the window? Maybe, maybe not. From time to time he still had that cold itchy feeling at the back of his neck.

He recalled the first time he had noticed it. That day he had paid no attention. And he fell into the trap of *ley fuga*. But he was one of the few to make it. Partly because he had been turned loose in a cemetery. Heavy gravestones provided a cover until he could reach the cemetery wall. But here he came face to face with another band of *soldados*. Don Benito had bribed these soldiers to shoot over his head. And Don Benito had provided him with money and a fast horse.

And he had come close to repeating the experience when he had tried to help Don Benito's widow regain possession of the rancho by enlarging her meager collection of diamonds with fakes made of paste. The plan backfired just as papers were about to be signed between the widow and the present owner of the rancho, an American with political connections. He had fleeced the young widow out of her holdings. Turn about was fair play, Lassiter reasoned. The rich American wanted to exchange the rancho for "Empress Carlotta" diamonds to give as a present to his mistress. But the gem artist who had faked the diamonds told his story for a price. Lassiter had to ride for his life.

He still intended to help Esperanza. Lassiter had promised Don Benito to look after the young woman should death overtake him. Lassiter had given his word. As he had given his word to Leland Ormsby that he would return with the cattle money. If the cadaverous old gentleman would chance losing nearly twenty thousand dollars by entrusting it to Lassiter, a stranger, then it meant he must have a lot more than that hidden around the ranch. Was that what Claire had meant about big money? Of course. She did know where the eccentric rancher hid his money. And she had told him that Leland Ormsby was practically reaching for the knocker on Death's Door. She had no idea what kept him alive.

Lassiter figured it was Claire in bed that made the old man want to cheat the grave as long as possible. Claire never said exactly what they did in his bed, not that it mattered. All Lassiter had to do was continue as foreman and stick it out for a few months until Ormsby just dried up and blew away. Even now he was only a husk of a man. Claire would inherit the ranch; Ormsby had promised it to her, she claimed. Well and good.

He looked over his shoulder at the distant town huddled beside the gleaming rails. No one was on his backtrail. He thought of the wreck. He didn't have much use for a company that allowed its roadbed to deteriorate to the point that it was vulnerable to flash floods so common to the area. He thought of the dead men with their Redgate map.

Long ago Lassiter had figured out the Redgate business. Someone with a macabre sense of humor no doubt had concocted a story of a Colonel Redgate who had vanished in the early days along with gold bullion looted from a Nevada mine. Gold intended to help the faltering South in the final days of the Civil War. But the conflict had ended just about the time Colonel Redgate and party reached this part of the territory, so the story went. Redgate and eight men, together with a mule train carrying the gold bullion, had simply vanished, as had the cavalry patrol later and the unfortunate Indians in search of white men's horses.

For a year or so the Redgate story would die down, then flare up again when the enterprising mapmaker would turn out a new batch, properly weathered and aged. The tale of Redgate gold in this territory vied in popularity with that of the Lost Dutchman Mine in another.

Lassiter experienced a sudden chill. While he had been ruminating over the stupid Redgate myth in order to keep himself awake, the sky had clouded over. He felt a sting of sand against his cheek as the wind came up suddenly.

The cutting edge of the storm blasted the bandanna he hastily tied over the lower half of his face. A vicious wind was now tearing at his black hat. He had anchored it by a thong under the chin, drawn so tight that it dug into the flesh. He squinted against wind-driven sand, seeking shelter. But the storm with its blowing sand and dust cut visibility to twenty feet.

The wind died suddenly, as it did on occasion, so that he was able to glimpse a hill dotted with rock and cactus. He urged the nervous gray horse in a desperate attempt to reach the lee side of the hill which would give him shelter. Something chipped a rock only a few feet ahead. A bullet? Lassiter strained his ears. Had he heard the faint crack of a rifle behind him in the distance? Or was the storm playing tricks with his imagination? He told himself this was no trick of the senses. Whoever was back there in the sand haze had meant the bullet for him.

Abruptly the wind slammed into him again. In the blinding gusts he missed the hill he had spotted. He rode on. After a mile or two of sheer horror, the horse faltered. But Lassiter kept it going. His lungs ached.

During a periodic lull in the storm when he could draw a fairly decent breath, he saw them. Three riders. So far back that he couldn't make out faces but there they were silhouetted against a rise of ground. He drew his gun, but the trio scattered to the shelter of low sand dunes before he could fire.

Then again the sand haze dropped like a curtain. Visibility was cut to ten feet.

"Tarsh, you sonofabitch!" he shouted at the wind, although he had no way of knowing for sure. One thing for sure, whoever it was back there wanted to get their hands on the satchel of money. What a fool he'd been to go along with Leland Ormsby's game of bringing back the money in cash instead of bank draft. Hell, he must have been thick in the head to agree to such a thing, whether the old man said gold was his luck or not.

That he had been broke and desperate at the time, Lassiter couldn't deny. Ready to try anything. He had money hidden in the wall of a certain house in Chihuahua, but there was no chance of getting his hands on it. Not now. Not after the trouble he'd stirred up down there on behalf of Don Benito's pretty widow. In time things might work out, but for the present it was proscribed territory for him.

As he pushed on he tried to take his mind off the trio on his backtrail, who were suffering as much as he. Hell, he'd survive this as he had other desperate games in life where the odds were not in his favor. Claire with her bright eyes danced across his mind. Claire would inherit the Ormsby ranch. It would be a place for Lassiter to let down for a spell after the hectic life he had been leading of late. Nice to have a woman and plenty of money and a cattle ranch to restock and manage. When the whole thing started to get thin, as it probably would, he intended to find her some man to take over. Lassiter would then turn his attention to helping Esperanza.

Lassiter grinned into the storm, pleased with the future.

Once, when the wind veered sharply, he heard the three pursuers shouting something. But he recognized nothing out of the garbled sound, distorted by the howling wind. Apparently they knew the area better than he did. At least one of them knew it better. Lassiter had only crossed this stretch of country twice, and that was when the air was calm, not whipped to a frenzy as now.

One of the pursuers with a superior knowledge of landmarks barely distinguishable in dust and sand, had gotten ahead of him. Lassiter glimpsed him in one of those shifts in the wind before everything closed in again. The man ahead was chunky, mounted on a dun. He was redheaded. Clothing and hat brim flapped in the wind.

When the sand closed in once more Lassiter swung wide in a circle instead of continuing straight ahead as the would-be ambusher obviously expected. All Lassiter wanted to do was get it over with. He didn't know whether this chunky man had become separated from the others in the storm or had simply ridden on ahead to get his bands on the money and the hell with the other two.

That was exactly what had happened, although Lassiter was only guessing. Eddie Danno had watched his chance and gotten away from Tarsh and J. D. Tramble. He knew the desert better than they did. They would probably die here. The sand would kill them. And Danno would have the satchel of money for himself.

Therefore he was surprised when Lassiter came riding at his back through a gap in the hills. Clumps of brush were in a wild dance under full force of the storm.

Danno jerked up his rifle, but too late. Lassiter fired. As Danno was slammed backward he managed to get off one rifle shot. It took Lassiter's livery stable horse under the left eye. The horse shuddered. Lassiter landed on a shoulder in the soft sand, rolled to his knees. He saw that the chunky man was down, unmoving. And the dun horse, stirrups flapping, was running away.

"Whoa! Whoa!" Lassiter shouted. He lunged in a futile effort to reach the animal. But it was pounding off into the dust, leaving him afoot. Lassiter tensed, wondering if the other two riders would appear out of the haze. But they didn't.

Lassiter looked at the man he had shot. A stranger. The man was dead. Lassiter then cut loose the satchel from the dead horse. Because the tempo of the storm had increased, he put the tarp over his head to keep the scythe of sand from ripping his face.

Weighted by the heavy satchel, he was winded before slogging half a mile through the drifting sand. Icy tension chilled the back of his neck. At any moment the other two riders might come up behind him.

The tarp over his head eased his breathing of dust-laden air. But a sudden wind gust whipped it away. Dropping the satchel, Lassiter made a frantic grab for it. But the canvas sailed into the dusty sky like a great graying bird. He hoped to find where it came to earth. But he had no more luck with the tarp than he had had in halting the dead man's runaway dun.

Even his bandanna was gone. He trudged on, fighting for breath, cursing the storm. At times the wind gusts staggered him. From a distance he might be taken for a drunk. Never had he been this unsteady on his feet, not even with a belly full of El Paso whiskey.

Whenever he risked a glance into the howling eye of the storm he saw nothing but a beige-colored curtain. How well-named, this stretch of terrible desert. The Furnace. When there was a momentary lull in the storm his reddened eyes searched for boulders, a ledge, a hillside, anything that would provide a landmark where he could hide the heavy satchel. He would come back for it later.

But would he ever be able to find it again? Then surely Leland Ormsby would brand him as a thief.

Twice he thought he heard horses behind him. Dropping the satchel he spun around, gun cocked. But there was nothing but bleak desert whipped by terrible winds. Lassiter tried to keep his back to the wind. The satchel was wearing him down. He spat out a mouthful of sand and attempted to get his bearings. But hills and mountains that might have given him a reasonable sense of direction were blotted out by the storm.

One of the greater hazards was the chance that he might use up his strength wandering in circles. Lassiter pushed the possibility from his mind, telling himself that his sense of direction was too finely honed for such a fatal mistake. However, a glimpse of the Santa Margaritas or the lower hills would be welcome.

He kept himself going by thoughts of the money that must be hidden around the Ormsby ranch; Claire said the old man never used banks that she knew of. When his tired mind balked at more thoughts of buried money, he turned to hot-blooded women such as Claire. He pictured that mass of black hair, the bouncy breasts with the kind of nipples he liked best. The pale skin and the tapered waist and lower down the dark patch at her fork.

"Claire, you steaming bitch, we'll spend old man Ormsby's money in the Sandwich Islands or Far China. And I'll plant your backside on the Great Wall and we'll make it shake."

He broke off, laughing wildly. Sand hammered against his teeth, the back of his throat. He was staggering. If he fell and struck his head on a rock, within seconds his mouth would be filled with choking sand. His long legs fought the storm as he plodded foot by foot, their muscles tough as the coiled springs of a bear trap.

He came abruptly over a hump of ground where cholla whipped by the wind looked like frantic old men waving their arms. And just as suddenly there was the hunched figure of a man with a gun. This was no illusion, but reality.

Three days after Lassiter had left with the OS herd, heading for the railroad and the cattle cars, Claire knew he would never come back. Leland Ormsby was a fool to trust him with the cattle money. She was more of a fool to have loved him. She was bitter. She sulked around the ranch house. Ormsby didn't seem to be paying much attention to her these days and instead retreated to the office where he kept his books on ancient Egypt. It annoyed her that he seemed obsessed with pharaohs, whoever they were.

And the skeleton crew Lassiter had hired and left behind offered no promise. Not a one of them would she risk with her great secret. Once in a while she would take her prize from its hiding place and study it. The prize in question was a Remington revolver so old it had been converted from cap and ball to cartridges. It was coated with cheap black paint on the grips and heel plate.

What had intrigued her was finding it in Ormsby's office. He had been examining the gun when she came in, fondling it almost. And later that day when she returned to the office, he was gone, but the gun was on his desk. He had forgotten to return it to the big safe where it was always kept.

What could be so important about an old gun that somebody had painted black? Ormsby evidently thought something of it because he kept it in the safe.

She took it to her room. Under strong daylight at her window she could barely make out a name on the heel plate where the black paint had worn thin. Sight of the name caused her pulse to leap. She thought of confiding in Joe Tarsh, who was foreman at the time, but knew from experience that amiable Joe could turn into a rattlesnake where money was concerned.

And then when Joe Tarsh was fired and Lassiter took over, she was filled with new hope. But then Ormsby had played into Lassiter's hands by allowing him to sell a herd of cattle. By this time Lassiter was no doubt sitting in some high stakes game using the cattle money.

Her luck changed. A new rider appeared at the ranch. She didn't know where he came from. He was tall and a little ravaged by the years, but still handsome. Ormsby was paying no attention to the new hands. And with Lassiter gone there was no foreman to check on things.

The new rider's name was Harry Benbow. Two days after his arrival, he and Claire went for a walk to the far side of the lake. Besides being a good lover, he wanted to know all about the ranch and about Leland Ormsby. She decided to trust him. She showed him the gun she had found and which Ormsby in his preoccupation with Egyptian history evidently had not missed. At least he had never mentioned it to Claire.

On the second evening she showed the gun to Harry Benbow. What had intrigued her about the man was the fact that he said he had once worked for the Pinkertons and now had a detective agency of his own in Nevada.

Benbow looked the gun over. "Let me take it to Tres Vidas. I know a man there who is an expert on such things."

"Can I trust you, Harry?"

"My darling, of course."

With her head spinning she believed him. Of course he could not match Lassiter when it came to the bombs going off, but what he offered was sufficient for the moment.

Her mistake was in stealing one of Ormsby's quarts of fine bourbon whiskey. Harry Benbow seemed dubious about taking the first drink. When she urged him on, happily, he sampled the bottle. Soon he got greedy. He staggered and began to sing in a loud and drunken voice. Claire, in alarm, tried to shut him up. The drunken singing attracted Leland Ormsby from the house and he crept up, bundled in a greatcoat and carrying a rifle. Fortunately Claire had put on her dress.

While she begged for her life and Harry's, the latter slipped away into the shadows. Ormsby finally ran out of breath.

"You hurt my pride with that drunken fool, Claire." She got the shotgun away from him, unloaded it and threw the shells into the trees. Then she helped him back to the house.

"I had counted on you joining me in a long journey, Claire," he said when they reached the house and he had recovered his strength with a brandy. "But now I don't know. I suppose you realize you are a sinful woman."

She said nothing. But he forgave her. She thought he might mention the missing gun, but he didn't. In the great bed she warmed him and cuddled him and soon he was snoring.

But the next day he fired all of the crew but two middle-aged cowhands. He said that if Harry Benbow ever returned he would shoot him. But Benbow didn't return. She was hurt when a week passed and there was no word from him. Some of her anger she directed at Ormsby. She didn't dare go too far, but she did mention Lassiter.

"I suppose you realize by now that Lassiter has double-crossed you with the cattle money."

"I don't think so, Claire."

He seemed so confident that she began to take heart. Two days later Harry Benbow sneaked back to the ranch. She met him outside. He looked awful, his eyes red, baggy, the mouth sagging. He admitted he had been on a drunk.

"That bottle of whiskey set me off." His hands shook.

"What did you do with the gun, Harry?"

"It's why I came back, Claire, to beg your forgiveness. I . . . I want to be fair with you."

"The gun. What did you do with it?"

"I pawned it for a bottle of whiskey. Down at Belleville. The owner of the saloon won't sell it back for less than a hundred dollars. If you can spare that much, Claire, I can buy it back."

"You'll use the money for whiskey."

"I swear on all that's holy that I will never take another drink as long as I live."

Claire was dubious but did give him the money out of her meager savings. He kissed her, smiled, and rode off. Whatever love for him had faded past; he was human wreckage.

Harry Benbow did plan to play fair with her. But on the way south to Belleville he stopped off at Tres Vidas for just one drink to quiet his nerves. By the time he reached Belleville a storm had come up. He barely made it. Sand shushed against the front of the saloon. Five miles back he had emptied the bottle of whiskey he had purchased in Tres Vidas.

"I . . . I wanna buy back that pistol." He had to hold onto the lip of the bar in order to keep his feet.

"It'll cost you fifty."

"You shaid it'd be onny tweshenty . . . twenty dollars."

"Have a drink, Harry, and then tell me what's so goddamn important about that old cannon."

But one drink was all it took. Just one more. Harry Benbow passed out cold. It was then that the full fury of the sandstorm struck the only building in Belleville.

Chapter Four

It was the same storm that had unhorsed Lassiter, had sent him staggering afoot for uncounted miles across the Furnace, carrying a brown leather satchel full of gold coins. And straight ahead of him was a man. The man was tall and very thin. He wore a Texas brush jacket and stood with his back to a sand hill which gave him slight protection from the wind. The hill was studded with rock. So far, he hadn't seen Lassiter.

The man had turned his head and was shouting, "Hey, I'm over here! By the hill! Got separated—" He broke off, coughing, then spotted Lassiter.

J. D. Tramble's sudden smile was vicious. A triumphant smile on the thin face that seemed to say he had Lassiter dead center and dead. And also he had the money all for himself.

In that flick of an eyelash in time, Lassiter flung himself across the dropped satchel just as Tramble's gun spat flame across the murky space that separated them. Even as he fell, Lassiter ripped up the .44. Off balance as he was, his own .44 slug struck lower than intended. It ripped into the upper thigh near the groin. Tramble screamed and staggered back a step, then fell. Lassiter reached him, searching the sandy air for the man's companion. But he saw nothing in the dimness. Lassiter threw away the gun the man had dropped.

"Where's your friend?" Lassiter demanded. "There were three of you bastards on my trail. I got one of you."

"Danno . . . he had big ideas." Tramble began to cough.

"Who's the third man?"

"Lost him . . . in the storm."

"Who is it? Tarsh?"

But the man shuddered there on the sand and died. This one was also a stranger.

"All right, Tarsh!" Lassiter shouted into the wind. "If you're the one, come and try to get this money. Try!"

A gritty wind hurled the words back at him. He started to repeat the challenge, then realized it was a waste of breath.

At least this dead hombre had had the foresight to anchor his big roan by the reins to a rock spire. It stood with rump to the wind, mane and ears flattened by the gale. Somehow Lassiter managed to lash on the satchel. He rode north, thankful to be on a horse once again. By the time the storm tapered off his strength began to return. His spirits lifted. Thoughts of a homecoming with Claire at the Ormsby ranch sent them soaring.

By the time the sprawl of adobe and red roof tiles could be seen through a forest of cottonwoods planted years back as windbreaks, the storm was dead.

But it had done its share of damage here at the northern edge of the Furnace. Two sheds and a privy had been tipped over. A corner of the bunkhouse roof was missing. And the trees that surrounded Ormsby's private lake were grayed from the same sand that coated the placid waters.

Sand was everywhere, on grass, roof tiles. One of the cowhands he had hired before leaving with the herd, came riding up from the bunkhouse to look him over. Mike Barlow's lined face showed surprise.

"Lassiter!" he cried. "You come across the Furnace? In that blow?"

"I did," Lassiter grunted.

"Wonder you ain't dead."

Lassiter didn't reply. He felt dead. Most of him did anyway. He slid to the ground and turned the weary horse over to Barlow.

"Me an' Bert Canfield are the only hands left," Barlow muttered. He glanced apprehensively at the big house. "That crazy Ormsby fired the rest of the crew you hired."

"He did, huh?"

"Jeez, I never recognized you at first, Lassiter. The dust an' all."

Lassiter climbed to the veranda and set the satchel down on a gritty table top. He tipped an olla hanging under the veranda roof and washed some of the dust from his face. He took a long drink, then looked at the house. Windows were covered with wrought iron as in Mexico. He lurched over to the heavy door and tried the latch. It was locked. He pounded on it with a fist.

In a few moments a wedge of Claire's frightened face appeared at a grille. Then she flung the door wide. "Lassiter!" she gasped, her eyes shining.

Standing on tiptoe, she reached for his mouth. "You taste of sand," she said.

"Likely I'll taste of sand from here on out. I swallowed a ton of it."

He stared through the open door into the gloom of a large parlor. He could see chandeliers and heavy Spanish furniture.

"The storm was terrible, Lassiter," she said. "You look like you rode through the eye of it."

"Where's the old man?"

"I think he's in his office."

"Why'd he fire most of the men I hired?"

"He's always been a little odd, but lately he's been, well, worse."

"You didn't answer my question. Why'd he fire everybody?"

"He even fired Mercedes. I've had to do the cooking." She met his bloodshot gaze and finally answered his question. "Leland got upset because one of the new men turned out to be a detective."

"How'd you know that?"

Claire fussed with a coil of thick black hair which was pinned at the nape of her neck. "Leland got suspicious and wormed it out of him. Harry Benbow was his name. He drank too much. Leland lost his temper and let everybody go but Bert and Mike."

"What kind of a detective was this Benbow?" Lassiter demanded, thinking that he might have been hired by Mexican authorities to track down a man named Lassiter.

Claire lowered her eyes. "He told me he used to work for the Pinkertons. Later he admitted they fired him because he couldn't stay away from whiskey."

"I must be losing my eyesight to hire a bum like that."

"He showed up here a couple of days after you left."

"What was he after?"

"Gosh, I don't know, Lassiter honey. He asked a lot of questions."

"Questions about what?"

"About Leland and how long he'd owned the ranch and where had he come from originally. Things like that."

Lassiter eyed her coldly. "And this Benbow decides to tell you his life story. About the Pinkertons and the rest of it."

She shrugged. She wore a gingham dress and looped earrings. "I got lonely and he was nice looking and—and I liked to talk to him."

"The truth is that old man Ormsby caught you two together."

"Nothing like that. I told you I'd wait for you, didn't I?" She tried to put on a show of indignation, but he was too weary to be impressed. He was wondering if she had tipped off Joe Tarsh that he was coming home via Andover instead of the San Pablo route to the north. She smelled good and he itched for her embrace.

"Tell me about the big money," he said.

"Do you realize this is one of the few times I've been outside the house since you left?" Claire said. "The place is like a fortress. With Mercedes gone, I've been trying to run things, but—"

"You're very good at other things," he said. She stroked the brown leather satchel that had been scoured by the blowing sand.

"What we could do with that cattle money," she said with a tight smile.

"Yeah. But it's the other money that interests me."

Wide green eyes studied him. "I really didn't know if I'd ever see you again, Lassiter."

"The money, damn it. Tell me."

"Is that the only reason you came back?"

He reached out and gently stroked her breast. "This too," he said with a hard grin.

She went over and closed the door, then led him by the hand down the steps and to the wall below the veranda. Here they couldn't be seen from the house. Her pinned-up hair accentuated a slender neck. "How I've ached for you, Lassiter."

He gripped the satchel while cocking a cynical eye at her. "You had the old man," he reminded her with a thin smile.

"Mostly my body warms him."

"And you found out he's got money buried around the place."

"I don't really know about that."

"The nearest bank is over a hundred miles north." Her evasions exasperated him. "You told me he hasn't left the ranch except to go to Tres Vidas. So what's he do with his dinero? Isn't that the big money you were talking about? *Isn't* it?"

"No," she said with a great sigh of relief, as if she had reached an important decision. "Meet me on the other side of the lake when it's dark."

"I'm counting on it. Give me a hint about the money."

She hesitated, then said excitedly, "Lassiter, don't look so skeptical. It's true about the money. Big money . . ."

A faint warning began to tick at the back of his mind. "If it isn't Leland Ormsby's buried money, then just what the hell kind of money are you talking about?"

"You act mad and you shouldn't be—"

"I didn't ride all this way to play games."

She hesitated, drew a deep breath, then said, "All right, I'll tell you." She looked over her shoulder, as if the secret about to be divulged was too important for other ears. No breath of air stirred the trees or rippled the surface of the lake. She turned back to him, her face flushed with excitement. "It's Colonel Redgate."

It astounded him so that he shouted the name. "Colonel Redgate?"

"Keep your voice down, honey. Gosh, we don't want the whole world to know."

For a moment he couldn't even speak. Then he said quietly, "You've got a map, I suppose."

She shook her head. "Not one of those fool maps. I mean the real thing, Lassiter. Colonel Redgate's million dollars."

"Redgate's gold," he muttered with a sour smile.

"A great treasure lost years ago," she went on in a breathy whisper. "At least a million in gold bullion from a Nevada mine. It was being brought by mule train—"

"Oh, sweet Jesus, no!"

"Listen to me, Lassiter," She gripped him by the arms, shook him. Dust rose from his shirt. "The colonel was trying to get money to the South. To help them in the Civil War. But on the way—"

"I know the damn story by heart." He shut his eyes, opened them, and a great bellow of laughter began to pour out of him. As the laughter continued, Claire seemed bewildered, then angered.

"I don't like to be laughed at!" Her green eyes smouldered.

He stopped laughing, licked some of the grit from his strong teeth, grinned. "It's all right, Claire. Hell yes, it's all right." Twice in the same year, he was thinking; paste diamonds in Chihuahua and now this . . . the Redgate million. "Soon's I see Ormsby, I figure to have a swim in the lake. Then I'll meet you in the trees on the other side." The sun was still high and they had plenty of time. She lost some of her anger, but still seemed upset.

"You sorry you laughed at me?"

"Sure."

"Why did you laugh?"

"I'll tell you about it later," was all he would say.

He walked tiredly to the bunkhouse, carrying the satchel. Barlow and Canfield were middle-aged cowhands, efficient enough for yard chores but not much when it came to a showdown with guns. That was Lassiter's assessment of the only hired help left on the place. The graying and nervous Barlow cooked him a meal. Canfield produced a bottle of whiskey. Hardly able to keep his eyes open, Lassiter tied the satchel to his wrist, lay down on a bunk. He placed his .44 at his side.

"Anybody tries to touch this bag while I'm asleep, and he's a dead man. You hombres understand that?"

"We ain't damn fools," the bald and lanky Bert Canfield said.

Lassiter didn't even hear him. He was already asleep. His recuperative powers allowed him to wake up refreshed after only three hours of sleep.

"The old man wants to see you soon as you come awake," Barlow said.

Lassiter washed his face in a tin pan, then took the money satchel up to the house. Claire and the old man were just coming out a side door. Leland Ormsby said something to her and she lost color. Lassiter realized she was actually afraid of the man.

Then Ormsby's skeletal features were grinning at him. "Welcome home, Lassiter."

"Isn't it good to have him back, Leland?" Claire said, her voice too shrill. Ormsby turned to look at her out of his vulture eyes and she went back into the house.

"I brought the money," Lassiter said, giving the brown satchel a slap that raised dust.

"So I see."

In the office set away from the house, Ormsby seated himself behind his flat-topped desk, looking like a withered doll. Lassiter put the bag on the desk, then slumped to the only other chair in the small room.

"You look as if you've been through hell and back," Ormsby observed as he opened the bag.

"It wasn't exactly a vacation."

Ormsby's withered mouth smiled. "Gold excite you, suh?" the Southern accent more pronounced than Lassiter remembered.

"Yeah, gold excites me."

"It is my life," the old man said, starting to laugh. Then his face suddenly paled and the lips twitched. He was hunched in the large chair, eyes closed.

"What's the matter?"

"I hurt now and then." Ormsby's bony hand waved him back. "An old Yankee bullet in the chest. Feels as if it moves occasionally." He began to count the money. It didn't take long. "All here, Lassiter. How much of the expense money do you have left?"

"Not a cent."

"You come right to the point, Lassiter. I like that in a man. And you'll have a thousand dollars bonus for returning the money to me." Ormsby counted out the thousand dollars, pushed the coins across the desk top. Lassiter scooped them up, dropped them into his pockets.

Ormsby placed the remaining money back in the satchel, then locked it in the big safe in the corner.

"And you have your job as foreman in addition to the bonus I gave you, suh." Ormsby sat down again. "Foreman of a ranch and no cattle?" Lassiter's smile was hard.

Ormsby did not respond. He gestured at the walls. "Soon I will leave all this. The house, the ranch. My lake. Did I ever tell you that I put in the lake because it reminded me of the bayous at home when I was a boy?"

"Interesting," Lassiter said. But it wasn't. He didn't care that the old man with the thickening accent had made his own personal bayou by damming a stream. He was impatient for darkness and the meeting with Claire.

"Ah put you to the test, Lassiter," Ormsby said.

"Three men trailed me out of Andover," Lassiter said when he had finally deciphered the syrupy accent. "One of them might have been Tarsh. I'm not sure about that."

"Ah got word to Tarsh that you, suh, would be coming back via Andover."

"I thought at first it might've been . . ." He didn't finish it. But the bright eyes told him the word omitted was Claire. Lassiter had told her as well as the old man of his plans. His jaw hardened. "So you admit a doublecross," he accused the old scoundrel who was smiling complacently from the big chair behind the desk.

"It was part of your test, suh."

"At least you don't try and lie about it." Lassiter eyed the big safe in a corner of the office, wondering how much was in there besides the cattle money. It didn't take him long to find out. There was a sound of horses. Barlow stuck his head in the door.

"Fellas from the bank, Mr. Ormsby."

Lassiter put his back to the wall, prepared for any eventuality. A big red-faced man with jowls Ormsby introduced as Oliver Morton of the Santa Rita Bank. Morton nodded, did not offer his hand. He seemed impatient. From what Lassiter could gather, Morton and the five men who crowded into the office with him had been staying in Tres Vidas. The bald Canfield had been sent with the word that Lassiter was back with the cattle money.

"I want to be on my way, Ormsby," Morton said crisply. He spoke of the storm, saying he hated this part of the territory for that reason.

"Ah told you Lassiter was a tough man and would return with the money." Ormsby grinned.

Morton turned and looked Lassiter over, as did the five hard-eyed men who had been assigned by the bank as guards. "I could use a man of your talents, Lassiter," Morton said.

Before Lassiter could tell him that the last thing he wanted was a job as bank guard, Ormsby cut in quickly. "He is workin' for me, suh."

Ormsby reopened the safe, removed the money satchel. Morton hastily counted the money. He put all but two hundred dollars into a canvas bag stamped Santa Rita Bank that one of the guards was carrying.

Ormsby produced pen and inkwell and watched Morton sign a receipt for the money. Morton exchanged this for a mortgage which he marked "paid in full." He signed his name and gave it to Ormsby.

"I'll be on my way," Morton said. "Want to cover as much ground as possible before sundown."

"Ah understand, suh."

"You've quite an accent. I didn't notice it when you came up to the bank last year for a loan."

"For some years ah tried to hide it. Now it no longer matters." Ormsby seemed amused.

Morton gave him an odd look, then said, "I will be glad to get out of this country for more reasons than one. My bed at the hotel in Tres Vidas was like a board and the food in town gave me a sour stomach."

"Ah suppose ah should have asked you all to stay heah."

"Yes, you could have," Morton snapped. He gave Lassiter a curt nod, then departed with his five men. Soon their horses could be heard pounding away from the ranch. Lassiter also wondered, as had Morton, why the banker and his entourage had not been invited to stay at the house while awaiting the return of a man named Lassiter.

He sat down again and watched Ormsby toying with the two hundred dollars in gold coins that Morton hadn't required for full payment of the loan on the OS ranch.

Ormsby found Lassiter looking at him and smiled. "You are now in possession of more gold coins than ah am. You have a thousand. All have two hundred."

"Plus a barrelful you've probably got locked up in that safe," Lassiter said, deciding to play along with the joke.

"These are the only gold coins in mah possession, suh. And ah do have slightly under ten dollars in silver. But that is the sum total of mah wealth in coin of the realm, so to speak. Minted by the United States of America. By rights they should be Jeff Davis dollars." For a moment the old man sat brooding, as if lost in the past.

"Nothing can change the surrender at Appomattox. The Civil War is over and done."

Ormsby's thin face was so drained of color for a moment that Lassiter thought he might collapse. "Suh, it was the War Between the States. And as for Lee's surrender, it was a disgrace. He should have fought on. Help was on the way. A million dollars could have sustained him through the summer and—" He broke off, the mouth in the thin face twisted in bitterness. "But the fool didn't wait."

Lassiter was curious enough to speculate on the old man's rather odd admission of his financial state. "You offered me a job as foreman. Where do you figure to get your hands on enough money to restock this ranch?"

"Ah have no coin of the realm, suh, only—"

"So you said. But I don't know whether to believe it or not." In all his years of knocking around the West, Lassiter had never encountered anything quite like this strange little man with the bright eyes. "A ranch without cows isn't worth a damn. And you sure don't have any use for a foreman if there's no cattle."

"Ah have need for you in other matters."

Lassiter almost laughed. "How do I earn my money?" He was wondering what additional lies would fall from the wrinkled lips.

"Ah have sold off all the cattle, suh. Most of the horses. Not yours, of course."

"Of course," Lassiter said. He started to get up, but Ormsby's next words stopped him.

"Ah want my heir to take over here, suh. Bare land. Let him fight his way up from the bottom. If he has the Yankee guts to do so." Ormsby stared at the wall.

Talk of an heir was a surprise to Lassiter because Claire was certain the old man would leave the ranch to her. She was counting on it. "Who's this heir you mentioned?"

"Ma grandson!" Ormsby uttered his old man's cackling laugh. "By the time he arrives, all will be gone. The pharaohs of ancient Egypt knew how to prepare for the afterlife."

Lassiter, who believed in this one life to be lived fully, looked at the shrunken face. "Pharaoh," he muttered with a shake of his head.

"A fortuneteller once told me that gold is mah luck—here and hereafter. Ah want you to participate in mah burial ceremony . . . it is why ah put you to the test."

"Digging graves isn't my specialty, old man."

"Mah tomb is prepared. Mah coffin is on slabs of granite. Ah will be buried with mah saber an' mah guns."

"Fine, fine."

"Do you know that the handles of mah coffin are solid gold?"

"Well, well."

"Don't grin, mah boy."

"I'm not a boy, Ormsby."

"When you're mah age, anyone under forty is a boy." Ormsby folded thin fingers at the edge of the desk. "You have passed the test. And for that you shall be rewarded."

"Being foreman of a ranch with no cattle and only a few horses doesn't sound like much of a reward to me." Lassiter had an urge to clear out, but he was intrigued. Damned if he wasn't.

"The offer of a job, suh was only bait. You were havin' bad luck at the time."

"It hasn't improved a hell of a lot."

"You have a thousand dollars."

"I damn near died for it."

Ormsby's parchment-like skin crinkled in a smile. "You survived, suh. You're a tough man. An honest man. You did return with mah money."

"I gave my word."

Spittle appeared at a corner of Ormsby's mouth. "Ah want mah grandson to have nothin' but a roof over his head. Ah hated his father—mah own son. Ah still hate him even though he is dead." Ormsby put a hand to his chest. "He . . . he fought for the Nawth. For all I know, it is his bullet in mah chest. Mah own son fought against me."

"I figured your friend Claire would inherit everything," Lassiter said tentatively.

"She will go on a long journey, suh and have no need for material things."

For a fleeting moment Lassiter wondered if the demented husk of a man huddled in the oversized chair intended that Claire be buried with him. But that was too far-fetched. He'd had enough of Ormsby. Again he started to get up.

"Ah could leave you a million dollars that ah do not intend my heir to have."

Lassiter almost laughed; he was still tired, still frustrated. "Don't tell me you got hold of a Colonel Redgate map."

"Suh, ah am Colonel Redgate." Ormsby wore a half-smile when Lassiter stared at him in amazement. To Lassiter, the name Redgate was like an Indian war drum inside his skull. He was sick of hearing it.

Ormsby said, "Some friends and ah looted the Empire Mine and—"

"I know the story," Lassiter snapped, his gaze on the pitiful looking figure behind the desk. "I've heard it fifty times. I've seen a dozen maps. I'm in no mood for jokes."

"Suh, aren't you goin' to give me the courtesy of listening?"

"You can't tell me one damn thing about Colonel Redgate that I don't already know."

"Ah ask you to believe ah am the colonel."

Lassiter reminded him of the day they had met. "I had just knocked down an hombre and his friends who had tried to sell me a Redgate map. Don't you remember?"

"Ah ask you to believe." Ormsby was trembling, the lips ashen.

"All right, you're Colonel Redgate, alias Ormsby." Lassiter stood up.

"Ah assumed the name Ormsby afterward. Ah remembered it as the name of a way station in Nevada."

"I'll leave you to your dreams, Ormsby." Lassiter turned for the door. Ormsby's sharp voice halted him.

"You don't believe one word ah have said."

Lassiter sighed, feeling a shred of pity. "Sure I believe you. Like I believe that an hombre out in San Francisco is emperor of California. He calls himself Emperor Norton and most people let him have his little joke."

Ormsby shouted at him. "Joke? You call what ah have told you a joke?"

"Don't get so excited. That old bullet in the chest might move in the wrong direction, Colonel." Lassiter decided to humor him with the military title.

Ormsby beckoned with a bony finger. "Come closer. Ah want to show you something."

Deciding to humor him one last time, Lassiter walked to the desk where Ormsby had spread out a paper.

"What is it?" Lassiter asked, for the light in the late afternoon was beginning to dim. Lassiter halfway expected it to be one of the Redgate maps. But it was a mechanical drawing of some kind.

"Lean closer, if you will, suh. Put both hands on the desk top so you can study it."

Lassiter leaned down, shook his head. "As I said, I'm in no mood for games."

"This is no game," Ormsby snapped. "This is a drawing of a special weapon. Made for me by a craftsman."

Lassiter felt a chill of apprehension. He didn't move a muscle but stood hunched over the desk top. "Go on," he said, "tell me the rest of it."

"That weapon is under mah desk. A revolver in a special frame. With a hair trigger. All ah have to do is touch it with mah foot. If ah do, you are dead. So do not move. Do not even twitch."

Lassiter held his breath. Now that he studied the paper more closely he saw that it was indeed the drawing of a cocked gun, or a lever that activated the trigger.

"Lassiter, you the same as called me a liar!" Ormsby glowered. "Worse, you compared me to that demented fool in San Francisco, Emperor Norton."

"I apologize," Lassiter said carefully.

"Too late. Ah revealed mah identity. Ah trusted you. You passed the toughest test ah could devise. And now you die!"

Lassiter flung himself aside just as a tremendous explosion seemed to lift the desk some inches off the floor. Concussion slapped at the walls of the small room, the single window rattling in its frame. Lassiter struck the floor hard. His eardrums ached from the great roaring. In one bound he was up, his .44 cocked and leveled at Ormsby trembling in the big chair. "Don't kill me, Lassiter." Obviously the weapon under the desk was a single shot.

"You crazy old bastard," Lassiter panted, "you're not worth killing."

"You hurt mah pride and ah wanted revenge. But ah am over it now."

Lassiter was staring at the hole in the desk top the size of his clenched fist. Canfield and Barlow burst into the office and looked wildly around.

"Heard a shot," Barlow said nervously. "What happened?"

Lassiter stepped outside to escape the cloud of powdersmoke boiling in the office. He drew fresh air into his lungs, then told the pair of cowhands about the gunshot.

"Stay around if you want," he said sharply. "Was it me, I'd hit the trail."

The two men exchanged baffled looks. Lassiter went to the corral. He was just saddling the horse he had left behind when cattle were shipped, when Claire came at him, dark hair spilling over her shoulders.

"At first I thought you'd shot Leland," she gasped.

"It was the other way around—almost."

Her jaw dropped when he mentioned the trick gun, but she got hold of herself and said, "What are you going to do now, Lassiter? Where are you riding to?"

"I'm pulling out. I've heard all the funny stories I can take for one day."

"But the money, Lassiter." When she tried to cling to his arm, he brushed her hand aside. "The money is here, Lassiter. Someplace. Believe me!" She seemed close to tears, but Lassiter was unmoved.

He rode away, Claire screaming at him to come back.

Chapter Five

Claire recovered from her shock of Ormsby trying to kill Lassiter with that trick gun. She knew about the weapon, having seen it a number of times: an ugly-looking instrument that could take a man's life as quickly as she could snap her fingers. She commandeered a saddle from Mike Barlow and rode after Lassiter. Only because Lassiter had kept his mount to a walk was she able to catch up to him.

She reined in, hair and eyes wild. "Listen to me, Lassiter. I had proof, real proof about Redgate."

"Had proof? Which means you don't have it now." He thought of spurting his horse, but he was in no mood for a hard ride after having experienced the hell of the Furnace.

"Proof that there really was such a person as the colonel." Quickly she told him about the gun coated with black paint and how Ormsby had left it out of the safe. "It was one of his poor days and he didn't want me that night. So I took the gun because I was curious. I asked myself why Leland would keep an old black gun in his safe."

He turned in the saddle and looked at her closely. She hadn't taken time to change and the dress was hiked up her legs. Equally provocative was a twitching of breasts caused by the high-stepping dun she was trying to hold in. "Why didn't you tell me about the gun before this?"

"You didn't give me a chance."

He slouched in the saddle, black hat tilted over one eye as the front of her dress continued to fascinate him.

She explored her own theory about the gun; Ormsby had stumbled onto it. Which meant it must have been found on the ranch. "He never leaves except to go to Tres Vidas."

"He went to Santa Rita last year to borrow money at the bank there."

"That was before I moved in."

"You're a sight, Claire, in that tight green dress."

"Here I come riding out to find you and . . . well, it's dangerous for a woman alone. I could be raped and you just sit there with that damnable grin."

He cocked an eye when she broke off and looked at him intently as the horses moved across the summer grass. The tip of her tongue slid across moist lips.

He said, "Rape is when a woman doesn't want it. And you do. It shows in your eyes."

"You make me sick—so smug and conceited." But her voice was shaking and her eyes had come alive, this time with more than her previous anger. The sun dipped under a cloud. Dust from the recent storm suddenly lifted from the leaves of tall cottonwoods as birds, disturbed by their approach, took flight.

When Lassiter reached out and lightly brushed one of her breasts with the tips of his fingers, she shivered, teeth sunk into her lower lip.

"How I've wanted to touch something soft," he said quietly. "All I've had lately has been a cattle car, hard seats and a long ride. There's a hotel in Tres Vidas."

His suggestion seemed to anger her. "You think I'd go there with you? Like a common . . . prostitute?"

"What the hell gave you the idea I was going to pay you?" he asked innocently. "Whores do it for money. This is for love." His sudden howl of laughter helped release knots of tension.

She gave him a sulky, sidelong look. Then a faint smile surrounded the tip of her pink tongue. "I can't risk staying away from Leland long enough to ride to Tres Vidas and back. But . . ." She gestured gracefully at a grassy stretch of ground some fifty yards from the ranchroad.

"Yeah," he said with a grin and reined his horse in that direction.

"If I do this, then will you listen to what I've got to say?" she wanted to know.

"I'll be so busy I might not hear much of it." Another bark of laughter erupted. "But you can talk all you want, Claire."

The grass here, though thinner than the plot at the lakeside, would do even though coated with dust from the storm. When he helped her dismount, she came lightly into his arms.

A faint hum of running water sounded from the trees. After tying the horses to a stump, out of sight of the road and a narrow plank bridge, he took her by the hand. A small stream trickled through spindly cottonwoods, the runoff from Ormsby's man-made lake. At one time there had been a full flowing creek before the rancher had erected his earth and rock dam to form the body of water he claimed reminded him of bayous when he was a boy. A few yards north of where they had stopped the stream meandered along a dry wash with sand banks some four feet high. But here it was on level ground.

"I need to get cleaned up," Lassiter grunted. After pulling off his dusty clothes, he plopped down in the streambed. The cool water was soothing. He let Claire wash his back, torso and long muscled legs, using sand as a substitute for soap to scrape off three weeks of accumulated grime.

While he washed off the sand, she removed her dress and lay back on it on the grass. A latticework of sunlight and shadow through overhanging branches touched her bare flesh.

She watched him step from the creek. "I want you to remember one thing, Lassiter. This is the first time I ever ran after a man."

"Must be my charm."

"You are conceited, you really are." But she smiled as he came striding toward her, a gladiator ready for combat.

When he knelt down she couldn't resist reaching out for his shoulders. She gripped him hard and her eyes burned into his face. He kissed her, softly at first, then deeply. Her mouth moved under his and her breathing quickened. After a moment she pulled away, gasping.

"I . . . I guess that's what I like about you, Lassiter. You're so damned sure of yourself."

"I've been hungry for this," he said against her breasts. "Over three weeks of hunger."

"No other woman in that time, Lassiter?"

"Too busy with cattle. Too busy making sure somebody didn't try and blow out the back of my head."

"Poor darling . . ." Then she shuddered as his body blotted the sun from her face. "You think you've been only hungry, Lassiter? I've been starved."

Her active participation made him believe what she had said. It was as he had imagined so often during those long nights and some of the days. Her long and lively legs, the warm, eager mouth, Because he was still slightly put out that she had led him on with that foolish Redgate business, he intended at first to make their reunion for his pleasure alone. But her pleasure was so obvious that he relented. Finally her teeth drew blood at an earlobe and her nails dug into his shoulders and back.

"Lassiter, Lassiter—what a team we make. It's never been like this with anyone. Ever."

It was five minutes before she recovered sufficiently so as to be able to talk about the gun without her voice shaking. "I kept the gun because I wanted to show it to you when you got back and—"

"Well, show it to me."

"It . . . it's gone."

"Proof of the pudding, as they say. And you don't have any proof."

"There you go again, not believing me. Now listen." She was struggling into her dress as she told him abort Harry Benbow who had been a Pinkerton detective and now operated out of an office in Nevada. "He's plainly and simply a drunk."

"Just tell me what happened to the damned gun."

"Harry admitted he traded it for whiskey down at Belleville."

"He picked a great spot to get drunk in. A wonder they didn't nail him to the privy wall."

"I gave Harry what money I had to buy back the gun. I haven't seen him since."

He made no reply to that. She needed a man and Benbow came along at the right time. The rest of it was just one more tall story. "You better come back to earth, Claire. Ormsby's crazy and it's starting to get to you. Clear out of this country before you lose the rest of your brains."

"Let me tell you something about that gun, Mr. Know It All. If you hold the gun just right in the sunlight you can barely make out a name on the heel plate."

"Let me guess. Colonel Redgate."

"Yes, but don't look so smug. Harry Benbow covered it with some black paint he found in the barn, just so no one would get curious."

He laughed again and she screamed at him and began to cry. He said nothing until she ran out of tears and rage.

"Take a stage out of Tres Vidas," he advised her grimly.

He gave her a hundred dollars of the money he had gotten from Ormsby. Then he rode her back within sight of the ranch house, with her arguing and pleading with him all the way. But he wanted no more of the mythical Colonel Redgate.

She gave him a smoldering look. "You should stay and help me, Lassiter. Now I'll have to make up a lie to tell Leland. I'll say I went after you because I thought he would want you to come back, no matter what."

"After trying to shoot off my head? You tell a good story, Claire. I'll say that for you."

Claire swore at him, crying again, and jerked so hard on the reins that the horse reared. It was at a gallop, the last he saw of her, skirts and hair blowing.

As he rode toward Tres Vidas he tried to make up his mind where to head next. He needed a stake. Tucson, perhaps, where they had some big games. With luck he could build that money Ormsby had paid him into something respectable. Then he grinned sourly at the late afternoon sky. So far all his plans to help Don Benito's young widow had blown higher than the moon. But he wouldn't give up. He owed too much to Don Benito's memory. And with Don Benito in his grave there could be no possible barb of conscience when it came to comforting a lonely and very attractive widow. Just contemplating such a future was enough to lighten his mood.

Just ahead was Tres Vidas and its cantina with thick adobe walls. He thought of the whiskey that would cut through the sand that still seemed to clog his throat. Whiskey could give a man the blessings of renewed life.

A man on the loafer's bench in front of the store leaned forward to stare at Lassiter and speak through a tangle of gray whiskers. "Didn't I see you over east about noon? You come ridin' outa the Furnace. You must've crossed it in that big blow we had."

"I crossed it," Lassiter said and heard the man say to other occupants of the bench, "Two of 'em in the same day. Ain't many make it outa the Furnace when the winds howl like they done today."

As Lassiter dismounted and tied his horse in front of the cantina, he wondered who the other person was who had made it out of the Furnace that day.

He didn't have long to wonder. As he started to shove his way through the swing doors he heard a familiar voice inside. ". . . Got separated from Danno an' Tramble, Lassiter, the sonofabitch, is likely dead in the sand along with them. I damn near never made it outa the Furnace myself."

"Wrong on one count, amigo," said Emilio Ruiz, the owner-barkeep.

"How's that?" Joe Tarsh snapped.

"Lassiter's lookin' at your backbone."

Tarsh dropped his glass. It rolled across the hard-packed dirt floor spewing whiskey. Tarsh started to spin around.

Lassiter said, "Touch that gun and you'll have no legs. I'll take my time shooting my way up to your head."

Tarsh looked carefully over his shoulder, his dusty face losing color. He was bareheaded. Long pale hair was still in a tangle from the wind. Specks of sand clung to his blond mustache. He bit one end of the mustache in frustration but made no move toward the big gun at this belt that was covered by a piece of canvas, tied on to keep off blowing sand.

"You'd play hell drawing that gun," Lassiter taunted. "Might as well have it in a gunnysack."

"Only take me a minute to untie it, damn you."

"Forget it." Lassiter added thinly, "I should put a hole in your head because of all the hell you caused me."

Ruiz placed hands that looked big as udders firmly on his bartop. It was said that his great uncle was a maker of maps and other spurious documents. The six patrons in the cantina edged out of the possible range of fire. No panic, just quiet observance out of eyes that had seen it all. The cantina smelled of sweat and beer and the raw whiskey Tarsh had just spilled.

"One of you two hombres shoot out my backbar mirror," Ruiz said, hunching big shoulders, "an' I skin his butt."

"Set out a bottle instead." Lassiter holstered his gun. "Might as well include Tarsh. He looks like he could use a drink."

Tarsh seemed to lose some of his tension. "You lead a charmed life, Lassiter," Tarsh said grudgingly.

"Two of your friends, didn't," Lassiter said quietly.

"You kill 'em? Or was it the storm?"

"Go back to the Furnace and see."

Tarsh thought about it, then said, "Too bad we didn't team up instead of tryin' to kill each other off Damn it, any man who can survive the Furnace is somethin' special."

"First thing you've said I agree with."

"You beat the Furnace. An' so did I."

Lassiter drank the whiskey Ruiz set out for him. It was a better quality than the gut-eater he'd had on the previous visit when Lassiter had lost his temper because a slicker and friend tried to sell him a Redgate map. The incident had led to the job with Ormsby. Not that it had meant much, only a thousand dollars and a lot of grief. Lassiter reminded him of that day.

"I think the old man was onto me usin' a running iron," Tarsh said with a tight grin.

"So you admit you were stealing his beef." Lassiter gave a shake of his head. "No wonder Ormsby wanted you fired."

"For that and other reasons."

"Yeah," Lassiter grunted. He knew he meant Claire.

Tarsh leaned close. "Let's split the Ormsby cattle money. It'll give us a stake for somethin' bigger."

Lassiter's jarring laughter caused Tarsh's face to redden. "Even if I had the money, you think I'd split with you?"

"It's likely in his safe. There's dynamite in a shed. We can blow the safe sky high."

Lassiter told him about the man from Santa Rita. "It'd mean jumping a banker and five bodyguards. And I've had enough of Ormsby money to last me a spell. You ask me, it's bad luck."

"I'm flat broke or I'd be miles from here. The old man must've paid you for the job you done. All right, we'll split that and I'll show you . . ."

Lassiter cut him off. "You take me for a generous soul, my friend."

"We can cross the border at Andover. I heard about three thousand head of beef just across the line. We'll hire some vaqueros an' move them cows to Sahuaro Junction. That cattle buyer's goin' to hang around there for a spell."

Lassiter showed his teeth. "I figured you were in Andover when I came through there."

"I didn't count on the train gettin' wrecked. All I wanted was the money sack. And then—well, hell, Lassiter, I admit I heard a certain Americano in Chihuahua would pay five thousand for your hide. It would've been a good day's work." Tarsh seemed proud of himself.

"You admit everything, don't you? A remarkable man."

A corner of Tarsh's mouth lifted under the mustache. "If we're gonna be partners, we can't have secrets."

"Who said anything about being partners? Where were you and your two friends when that pretty gal put on a show for me in the hotel window? Hiding under the bed?"

"Ruby's a friend of mine," Tarsh said. "You told her you'd be back. We waited. But not too long."

Lassiter had to smile. He sipped his drink and looked Tarsh over. There was something almost likeable about the big blond man with the diamond chip blue eyes. But he wouldn't trust him any farther than he could throw a fistful of straw into the maw of a sandstorm.

Tarsh was saying, "You stay workin' for Ormsby an' you'll turn up crazy as he is."

"I quit."

"Then come in with me." Tarsh sounded eager. "We can clean up an' head to California an' spend our money."

"I'm kind of fond of my head, Tarsh." Lassiter touched his own skull.

"What you mean by that?"

"If I went in with you, my head might end up in a gunnysack that you'd trade for five thousand American dollars across the line."

Tarsh looked aggrieved, met Lassiter's hard grin, then shrugged and laughed. "Yeah, well, I'd likely have done that before I got to know you better. But I kinda like you, Lassiter. We'd make a good team."

"I've had enough of this part of the country. I'm moving on."

Tarsh thought about it. "Figure to take Claire along?"

Lassiter shook his head. "I gave her some advice. To get away from Ormsby."

"But she won't. She wants that ranch when the old man dies."

Lassiter almost mentioned that the old man had named a grandson as his heir. Then he decided to keep his mouth shut. It was none of his business, nor was it Tarsh's. If Claire was fool enough to believe everything Ormsby told her, then she was going to come up short in the game. He had wanted to warn her, but all she would talk about was Redgate gold. He was heartily sick of it.

"And sick of Ormsby," he added aloud. He told Tarsh about the old man's attempt to kill him with the hair-trigger weapon under the desk.

"You're lucky you smelled trouble," Tarsh said. "Don't know how many men Ormsby killed with that trick gun. Three since I went to work for him. Killed 'em one at a time. Was my job to bury 'em."

"They say that cold-blooded murder can get you life in the Fortress," Lassiter said. "And that's worse than hanging."

Tarsh shrugged it off. "Like the man said. Ain't what you do, it's what you get caught doin'."

Lassiter finished his drink and then drew his .44 in one smooth movement. "I'll take your gun, Tarsh."

"The hell—" Tarsh froze as Lassiter ripped free the lashes holding the canvas dust guard over the revolver. He drew the weapon, a .45 with walnut grips and stepped back.

Tarsh reddened and Ruiz behind the bar, stiffened. Two of the patrons paused with drinks halfway to their mouths. Tarsh said, "Thought we was friends, Lassiter."

"Halfway. But even good friends have been known to shoot other friends in the back. Specially in this part of the territory." Lassiter mentioned the bench in front of the Tres Midas store. "I'll leave your gun there."

He flipped a coin on the bar to pay Ruiz for the drinks. "All your worry about the backbar mirror, Emilio. Nothing happened. Nothing at all."

"You push your luck too far with hombres like him," Ruiz said in a low voice, nodding at Tarsh standing rigid down the bar, "an' you end up very dead."

"One day I will, no matter what happens. We all will," said Lassiter.

Chapter Six

Following his encounter with Joe Tarsh, Lassiter headed south. He found himself thinking of Claire's wild story about Harry Benbow and the Remington revolver. That first night he took supper with some freighters camped for the night. He casually mentioned Benbow, wondering if they had run into him.

"He's the hombre down at Belleville," said a big bearded man with suspenders over a dirty shirt. The man went on to say that Benbow, who claimed to be a former detective, was being kept in a drunken stupor at Belleville.

Lassiter asked questions and the man said, "We fust run into him out here on our last trip. Sorry-lookin' hombre. After we fed him he talked about chasin' thieves an' murderers while he was a Pinkerton man."

"A good story," Lassiter said, sipping coffee. "A lot of 'em around this part of the country, seems like."

"Benbow claimed his young wife run off with a neighbor kid. That's when he got to drinkin' so hard. Well, we was so interested in what he was sayin' that we didn't notice he drunk most of our whiskey."

Just for the hell of it, Lassiter swung farther west and cut for the border.

Belleville consisted of a single building owned by Dan Rambert, that housed a store, small dining room and a large saloon and dance floor. There were rooms upstairs.

Two girls were lounging at an empty table when Lassiter walked in. A tall barkeep with thinning hair and long sideburns, wearing a green vest, smiled pleasantly. "Your pleasure, sir."

"Whiskey." Lassiter sipped his drink and listened to four customers at the end of the bar talk about moving cattle from one side of the border to the other, something Joe Tarsh had suggested. He doubted if Harry Benbow was one of them; Benbow who had pawned a gun that Claire thought was important.

The only other person in the long room was an old Mexican in a faded red shirt. He stared vacantly at the wall while doing something to a guitaron, his fingers working slowly and methodically on the stringed instrument.

"If you wish to dance with one of the young ladies," the barkeep said politely, "Abron will be finished replacing the broken string in a minute."

Lassiter shook his head. "I need a spare gun," he said confidentially. "But I don't want to spend much."

"My name is Dan Rambert and I am at your service, sir." A few strands of reddish hair were combed carefully across his scalp. Rambert was about thirty. He placed a small box on the bar that contained some weapons left in exchange for whiskey, among them a derringer with a broken hammer, an old Navy Colt.

Lassiter looked directly into Rambert's intelligent brown eyes. "That all the guns you've got?" He sensed the man was holding back.

"You looking for something special?"

"A gun that will shoot. I wouldn't trust any of those."

"Only occasionally does anyone leave a decent gun in lieu of a bar bill," Rambert explained as he put away the box of weapons.

Lassiter finished his whiskey. Claire had lied to him about the gun of course. He'd been a fool to ride out of the way just on the chance she might have been telling the truth. But then what about the freighters who said they had run into Benbow?

"Here's a gun I forgot I had," Rambert said and placed an oversized Remington revolver on the bartop.

An ancient weapon, its looks spoiled by a coat of cheap black paint on the butt. Lassiter pretended to check the heavy weapon for balance.

"Looks like a cannon," he said indifferently.

"Could blow a hole in a man as big as a bucket," Rambert said. The four men at the el of the bar at the end were watching Lassiter with the revolver. Even the two girls seemed interested. One was a plump and pretty brunette, the other thin and with ginger-colored hair. They wore spangled dresses, typical of dancehall girls.

In the silence, Lassiter said to Rambert, "How much you want for the gun?"

"A thousand dollars."

Lassiter smiled. "I can buy a second-hand Gatling gun for that much."

"No doubt." The urbane Rambert also smiled.

"Not much of a gun. Why the high price?"

Dan Rambert leaned across the bar so that Lassiter could smell pomade that kept the sparse red hairs in place. A fly on a dusty shelf noisily and desperately tried to free itself from a spiderweb. "When there seems to be a market for something I have for sale," Rambert said quietly, "the price goes up."

Lassiter decided to play another card. "The gun belongs to Harry Benbow. Used to be with Pinkerton."

"Private detective is the wrong business for a drunk."

"I'll buy the gun for a reasonable price and give it back to Benbow."

"You a friend of his?"

"I hear he's been hanging around here."

"That so?"

"I'll give you twenty dollars for the gun," Lassiter said. "Probably more than you loaned Benbow on it."

"I gave him fifty."

"Damn generous." Lassiter was wondering if he had stumbled onto something after all.

Down the bar the four customers still stared, big men in partial shadow, dressed as cowhands. A late afternoon sun through a high window touched the crowns of their hats.

Rambert said, "Mister if you're not interested in the gun, take it back." He extended a hand for the weapon.

"All right, I'll give you fifty," Lassiter said with a shrug. He knew Rambert by reputation; cold steel under a smooth facade, a former professor of Greek history, it was said, who fled west because of a shooting scrape. Rambert watched Lassiter lay out five ten-dollar gold pieces on the bartop. Lassiter thrust the big Remington into his waistband.

"Benbow came back a week or so after he left the gun," Rambert said in his cultured voice. "Offered me a thousand for it. Wanted to give me an I.O.U. He was pretty drunk. I fed him whiskey. That ended him wanting the gun back. All he wanted then was more whiskey. I had a feeling somebody would come along and want to buy that gun."

"You didn't have too long to wait," Lassiter said, backing a step away from the bar. "Now I've got the gun. And you've got my fifty dollars."

In the tense silence the ginger-haired girl sprang up from the table and hurried upstairs. The plump brunette had stiffened in her chair, losing color. Long experience in such places had made her alert for trouble. And as the seconds ticked away, Lassiter and the saloon keeper locking eyes, two of the men down the bar left by a side door, one of them saying just before the door closed, ". . . Want no part of it." They rode quickly away.

Lassiter edged back so he could keep one eye on Rambert and also on the pair who remained at the end of the bar. He didn't discount the brunette, knowing from experience that a derringer could be hidden under a garter.

"Where's Benbow?" Lassiter asked crisply of Rambert.

"Mister, you haven't paid for your drink."

"Take it out of the fifty dollars," Lassiter said.

Hoofbeats from the horses of the fleeing pair had already begun to fade.

"Fifty dollars was for the gun only," Rambert said, his smile still in place.

"How much for the whiskey, then?"

"Nine hundred and fifty dollars. And two bits."

"You're being a little foolish about this, Rambert."

Rambert did not turn his head when he said, "You are the one being foolish, sir." He addressed the pair down the bar: "Brownie, Sam. I've done favors for you boys. Now I need one. I have a customer who refuses to pay for a drink."

"Keep out of it," Lassiter warned them flatly.

He backed toward the door which caused the brunette to squeal with fright and go bounding up the stairs to the second floor as the ginger haired girl had done.

"Took me awhile to recognize you, Lassiter," Rambert said. "Something familiar about you when you walked in. When you inquired about the gun, I got curious."

"Curious can get you dead. You know what happened to the cat."

Rambert showed his white teeth. "This is tough country. You could end up in the Fortress. Better to commit suicide, they tell me, than spend ten years in that prison."

"I'll take my chances."

"Makes more sense for you to pay up than make trouble."

He was interrupted by a sudden commotion upstairs. One of the girls was yelling. "I tell you it's true, Harry! A man's come for your gun. He bought it."

Then another voice, so thick with alcohol it was almost speaking a foreign language: "Ryan, by God it's Ryan. He followed me from Virginia City."

All eyes turned to a tall, loose-jointed figure in dirty shirt and pants, with hair badly in need of trimming, and a face which once might have been fairly handsome. He paused midway up the open stairway, clinging to the banister with both hands, staring down at Lassiter out of bloodshot eyes.

"You Benbow?" Lassiter called to him.

Rambert answered for him, laughing. "Former Pinkerton ace detective!"

Crouched on the stairs behind Benbow was the brunette. "You shouldn't pick on him, Dan. He's sick."

"Mollie, it's a sickness known as drunk," Rambert said.

Benbow stumbled on down the stairs and stood weaving while he tried to focus on Lassiter. "You're not Ryan!"

Lassiter beckoned. "Come along, Benbow. I'm taking you out of here."

"Ho, ho," Rambert chortled. "Brownie, you hear that? You hear what he said, Sam? He not only refuses to pay for his drink, but now wants to kidnap my star boarder." Rambert set a bottle on the bar, poured an inch of whiskey into a glass. He pushed it across the bar to Benbow. "Here you are, Harry. Your hourly drink."

Benbow staggered to the bar, leaned heavily against it.

Lassiter said, "Don't touch the drink, Benbow!"

Rambert lost his smile. "My nose twitches and that means I smell money. I think we all will have a talk with Lassiter and find out what this is all about."

Rambert was still speaking as he made an easy turn to grab a sawed-off shotgun from behind the bar. Brownie Lock and Sam Varney backed away from their el of the bar. Nearby, the old Mexican clutched the guitaron, looking blank and a little frightened.

In that split second Lassiter's left hand had already closed over a chair back. He hurled the chair overhand. It splintered against a forearm that Rambert flung up to protect his face. But impact knocked him backward and he crashed to the floor. Reflex action discharged the shotgun at the ceiling, tearing a large hole.

In the same movement Lassiter fired at Brownie Lock, the first man coming around the end of the bar. Above the roar of the .44 sounded his scream. He collapsed. Sam Varney saw the .44 swing to cover him. He froze, then threw down his gun and lifted his hands.

"I'm out of it, Lassiter! I'll wait till next time!"

With his hands still lifted Varney backed to the side door, his mouth twitching. Lassiter watched him bound into the saddle of a gray, ready to shoot him through a side window if he reached for a booted rifle. He didn't. He spurred away.

Drawing a deep breath, Lassiter looked over the bar. Lambert was out cold, bleeding from a gash the chair had put on his forehead. Lassiter, keeping one eye on the frightened brunette Mollie, unloaded the shotgun. He threw the shells to one side of the room and sent the shotgun crashing through a window. Then Lassiter inspected Brownie Lock. A bullet had smashed Lock's collarbone. He was well named, with brown hair and matching beard.

An ashen-faced Benbow had retained enough sense to fling himself flat when the shooting started. Now he got clumsily to his feet and clung to the barlip. When he tried to pick up the drink Lambert had poured for him, he dropped the glass.

Lassiter eyed the cowering brunette. "Who else is upstairs?" he demanded, gesturing with his gun at the second floor.

"Only Ginger. Take Harry with you. We've been trying to help him, but Dan keeps him drunk all the time. Harry's nice. He really is."

Benbow was staring owlishly at the Remington in Lassiter's waistband. "The Redgate gun . . ."

"You're coming with me, Harry."

But Benbow turned, nearly losing his balance, and pointed at the old Mexican who stood stiffly on a small platform beyond the dance floor. He still clutched his guitaron and was staring wildly around.

"He—he knew Colonel Redgate," Benbow was saying, his voice even thicker than before.

Lanka crossed over to the old man. "Don't look so worried," Lassiter said in Spanish. "I'm not going to hurt you. What's this about Colonel Redgate."

"I saw him, senor, when I was a young man," the Mexican said, eyes staring blankly in Lassiter's direction. For the first time Lassiter realized he was blind.

"You don't have your sight, yet you saw Colonel Redgate?"

"At that time I had my sight, senor."

Lassiter was skeptical about Redgate. "Can you remember what he looked like?"

Alejandro Abran said that the colonel was an older man, even back then, with gray mustache and full beard. Abran now was also gray in the head but probably no more than forty. "I had a herd of goats up on the mesa," Abran said as he spoke of his one and only meeting with the mystery colonel. "There were nine in his party, counting the colonel. Many mules, some with heavy loads."

Lassiter tried to read something in the sightless eyes and failed. For sure, there was little to read on the lined and leathery face. "He *told* you he was Colonel Redgate?"

"Introduced himself, senor."

"And you say he had mustache and beard?" Lassiter prompted, trying to relate the elusive colonel with the emaciated smooth-shaven features of Leland Ormsby. It was impossible.

"A fine-looking man," Abran said. "But there was something in his eyes that put a chill in my spine."

"How long ago was this?"

"While you Anglos were fighting your great war."

"Civil War, you mean."

"He spoke of it as the War Between the States. My cousin and I, we slaughtered goats and fed the colonel and his party. We were afraid not to."

"Anybody else with you but this cousin?"

"No, senor."

"Did the colonel tell you anything about himself?"

"They packed up the leftover meat and rode away. It was the last I saw of him."

"Is your cousin still alive?" Lassiter hoped that a man who still had his sight might remember more. But Abran said his cousin had died some years ago. "Since shortly after meeting Colonel Redgate I lost my sight," said Abran, "when I was stricken with fever."

"Did you ever hear what happened to the colonel and his party?"

"Of course. A great storm buried them under tons of sand."

Lassiter mentioned the black-butted Remington that Harry Benbow referred to as the Redgate gun. "A gun with the colonel's name on it."

"I know about it," Abran said, turning his head to the sound of Lassiter's voice. "Great storms sweep the Furnace and the sand moves. Probably the gun that was lost for so many years was uncovered in a storm. Somebody found it."

"Yeah, maybe." Lassiter reloaded his gun. He was beginning to wonder if Leland Ormsby had done away with the colonel and now in his senility imagined himself to be Colonel Redgate.

Lassiter asked Abran if he had heard of Leland Ormsby. Abran nodded. Lassiter said, "Was he living around here when the Colonel came through?"

Abran shook his head. "There was nothing here then. I brought my goats up from Mexico because the grass was good on the mesa."

"You ever hear Leland Ormsby's voice?"

"At Tres Vidas. I am related to Emilio Ruiz and Senor Ormsby was a patron of his cantina. I played for dancing up there for a time. Senor Ormsby liked to dance before he became too old. I have not heard his voice for some years now. I came down here because I have many relatives across the border. They visit me here and it brings me pleasure."

Lassiter had a parting thought. "Any idea who makes the Redgate maps?"

Abran smiled. "I told my uncle the story of Colonel Redgate. My uncle was a sly one and made a map. A tenderfoot Yanqui paid him a hundred dollars for it. He made another and another."

"So your uncle's the mapmaker."

"Now it is his son. He makes too many." Abran chuckled. "But he has a fondness for American dollars."

Lassiter pressed a gold piece into Abran's hand. The blind Mexican felt of it with sensitive fingers and determined its value. "Ten dollars!" he exclaimed. *"Gracias!"*

"*De nada.*"

"I know there was trouble here. The girls screamed."

"They're all right. Not a scratch."

"And I heard shooting."

Lassiter told him about Rambert and the shotgun, the other man who had tried to draw a gun and about the one who had fled.

"And Senor Rambert?" Abran inquired. "I hope he is not dead. He has been good to me."

"He'll have a headache, for sure."

The girls were behind the bar, attending to Rambert who was sitting up, looking dazed. The brunette was sponging blood from his face with a wet towel. The other girl, thin and with ginger hair, glared up at Lassiter.

"A wonder you didn't kill him with that chair," she snapped.

"Better I should have let him blow me out of my boots with a shotgun?"

Lassiter walked over and looked at the injured man. He was unconscious. Blood had thickened in the area of his collarbone.

Lassiter got Benbow outside. The man carried a bottle, tying to hide it from Lassiter. Lassiter took it away from him. The bottle was nearly empty. "You were drinking all the time I was talking to the Mexican," Lassiter said.

They got Benbow's horse out of the stable and rode south into Mexico, along an old smuggler's trail Lassiter remembered.

"There's nothing to the Redgate story," Lassiter told him. He spoke of the blind Mexican. "He helps keep the legend alive with his stories about Redgate. And why not? His relative makes a living off those maps."

By then Benbow, so far gone he could not even talk, sagged in the saddle. Lassiter had to tie him in place. Just before sundown, with reds and golds washing the outer edges of a pueblo, Benbow's heart finally gave out. The whiskey he had gulped so greedily while Lassiter was having his discussion with Abran had done him in.

Lassiter paid two vaqueros to bury him, then rode on keeping his eyes open for rurales. So far as he was concerned, he told himself, the legend of Redgate was finished.

But next morning he was curious enough to use a pocketknife to scrape off some of the black paint, remembering Ormsby's fetish concerning gold. He was finally rewarded by a gleam of bright metal. And on the heel plate a name was etched: Colonel Redgate. It still meant nothing, really. He unscrewed the gun grips, thinking there might be something else etched on the undersides. But there was nothing.

He turned the gun grips over to a Mexican assayer who pronounced them solid gold. Lassiter paid the man for his services and thought about it as he rode south. Ormsby had said that gold brought him luck. But to have a gun with solid gold grips lying around was temptation to a thief. The perfect disguise was to mask it with a coat of paint. Ormsby in his fantasies had had someone etch the colonel's name on the heel plate. But whenever Lassiter tried to push the whole Redgate business back into his mind, it kept creeping back, demanding further inspection. But he refused to be swayed. To hell with it!

Chapter Seven

Earlier in the month Diana Ormsby told her husband that of all the places they had seen so far in the West, she was most taken with Virginia City. A slender, frail-looking girl, she had hair and brows the color of cornsilk and a mouth that could pout prettily or smile, depending on her mood.

Bruce looked as young and inexperienced as his wife. He tried to compensate for it by a jaunty air as he explained that Virginia City was not as prosperous as it had been in his grandfather's time during the war years. And thank God, at long last, Diana had found something about the West that she liked.

Diana was pleased that here the ladies were fashionably dressed and the men were gentlemen. Something she had not found in other frontier towns such as Omaha, the great jumping off place of the steam cars.

That afternoon they had checked in at the Comstock, one of Virginia City's more ornate hotels. Diana looked hopefully at Bruce as she started hanging up her satin dresses. "I'd love to make our lives here," she said.

"We have a ranch to take over," Bruce reminded her for the tenth time. Coming West had frightened him almost as much as it had Diana. They had been married a year, and so far neither had found the expected bliss. Bruce had been made a partner in the family textile business after graduation from the college at

Princeton. As expected, soon afterward Bruce and Diana were married. Bruce's father then died suddenly. In trying to run the business, Bruce learned that his father had invested heavily in linen, expecting it to replace cotton. It didn't. He and Diana were living in the family mansion at Washington Square when the bank foreclosed not only on the business, but the house as well. Diana's family had lost their fortune in shipping, a business that had never fully recovered after the war. Bruce got a job with another textile house but soon realized he knew little about fabrics; his father had kept everything to himself.

In his early years Bruce thought his father was his only kin. But when Bruce was ten his grandfather wrote a letter to Bruce's father, inviting them West for a visit. At first Bruce's father was angered, then resigned.

"After all, he is your grandfather—my own father," he said to young Bruce. "Sending him to prison would prove nothing after all this time. And we are rich enough as it is even without his damned Empire Mine. So he's alive. And I thought he was dead."

"What did grandfather do that was so terrible?"

"He wanted to save the South. He was a fanatic. But so was I for the North. Those were dark days. I'm glad you were too young to experience the blood and hatred."

Bruce was jolted back to the present when Diana said, "You could surely find something to do here. Virginia City is exciting. I just hate to leave."

Bruce groaned and looked at his pretty wife. She had celebrated her twentieth birthday on the trip West in a dismal frontier hamlet where the food at the railroad cafe was greasy bear steak, the wine nearly vinegar, and the hotel bed lumpy. Diana didn't complain, however. But she did wonder as she had before, what had ever made her think that marriages were made in heaven.

He reminded her again that his grandfather had handed him the OS cattle ranch. "I have to learn the business." His smile was stiff. "And you can learn to be a good ranch wife."

She sank to a needlepoint chair, thankful for the comfort, a contrast to being jolted and chilled and forced to breathe foul smoke from the locomotive for so many days.

She mentioned a map his grandfather had sent along with the quit claim deed and the rather strange request, really a command, that he change his name. "There is only one town, Tres Vidas it's called. It looks like a village. What will we ever do for fun?"

"After we're settled maybe we can go up to Santa Fe. And someday we might be able to visit the capitals of Europe."

"We just can't sit around waiting for him to die so we can inherit his fortune."

"Diana, I will make it on my own." He faltered. "Well, I am going to try at least."

"You said your father once spoke of your grandfather as touched in the head."

"Eccentric. A lot of people are." Bruce's encouraging smile wavered. Aside from one visit to his grandfather's ranch when he was a boy, all Bruce knew about the West was what he read in Apperson's Weekly.

"And this nonsense about changing your name," Diana said, "proves your grandfather is more than eccentric."

Bruce had to admit the truth of her statement. Changing the name was a condition of Bruce receiving a quit claim deed to OS ranch. He already had title and had legally changed his name and sent his grandfather proof.

Because Diana was worn out after their long journey, Bruce went downstairs to the saloon off the hotel lobby. A place with darkly paneled walls, bustling with well-dressed men who talked silver and gold and mines and railroads. All quite fascinating. He had several drinks.

A slender, well-dressed man with a nice smile, moved in next to him at the crowded bar and introduced himself as Gil Ryan. He was a reporter for the Territorial Enterprise, a few years older than Bruce. Ryan was slightly tipsy.

"I saw you arrive in Virginia City with a mighty attractive young lady on your arm."

"My wife."

"Oh. I am sorry," Ryan said, clucking his tongue. "I thought anyone that beautiful would be your mistress. Men make a habit of leaving wives at home when they visit Virginia City. I am sorry," he said again. "I see I've offended you. I'm a little too full of Comstock whiskey, I'm afraid. Let me buy you a drink. By the way, I didn't get your name."

"Bruce Ormsby."

They talked of fascinating Virginia City and after a few more drinks, Bruce tittered and said, "Tell you the truth, my grandfather was quite a figure in this place during the war."

"You don't say? My uncle was a nabob here at the time."

"He was connected with the Empire Mine."

Ryan frowned, leaned close. "You said—Empire Mine?"

"Yes." Bruce was pleased that Ryan seemed impressed.

"Small world, so was my late uncle up to his golden ears, as we say around here, in Empire stock. What was your grandfather's name, may I ask?"

"Redgate . . ." Bruce had a feeling he shouldn't have mentioned the name, but in his foggy state he couldn't quite figure out why.

"There was a Colonel Redgate."

"I am really Bruce Redgate but my grandfather asked—insisted that I change my name to Ormsby."

"Hmmm. Well, understandable. Ormsby, you say is the name he insisted you take?" But Bruce had disappeared in the crowd. Ryan was suddenly cold sober. There was a former Pinkerton man, Harry Benbow, who had opened an office in Carson City. Ryan intended to see him first thing in the morning. Perhaps this time the other stockholders of the defunct Empire Mine would listen to him. Most of the original stockholders were deceased, but there were descendants. Ryan himself was one.

"Jesus Christ—Redgate!" And everyone at the bar turned and stared at him.

When Bruce climbed the stairs to their room he found Diana at the window, watching the nightly parade along C Street. "I want to make our home here, Bruce," she said.

"Impossible. I'm going to bed."

"You're drunk."

"Pleasantly so." He told her about running into a newspaperman who seemed impressed when Grandfather Redgate was mentioned. "To come all this way and find someone who remembers that such a person as Colonel Redgate actually lived here!"

They argued about Virginia City, then finally retired. Diana had been taught that a wife's role was passive, although she had hoped it might be otherwise. A time or two she had actually tried to inject some enthusiasm into her nightly role as bed companion, which was how Miss Simkins at the academy for young ladies had once referred to the intimacies of marriage.

But Bruce was always finished with her before the possibilities of pleasure crossed her mind.

They had to delay their departure from Virginia City because Diana was indisposed after a rich meal at a restaurant near Piper's Opera House. Bruce thought it strange that she was able to walk the streets with him during the day, but even mention of the long stagecoach ride over rough roads that faced them seemed to upset her delicate digestive system.

Finally, he worried that his grandfather might think he was ungrateful and not coming West after all. He wrote, saying they had decided to spend some time in Virginia City. He thought it would please his grandfather.

Time and again, when Diana mentioned the dreaded trip south, Bryce explained that their only chance for survival in the West was to accept what his grandfather offered. There was no alternative. Staying in Virginia City was out of the question. At long last, a tearful Diana boarded a stagecoach that would take her to what she was certain to be the very end of God's earth.

Chapter Eight

Claire felt herself tense up with anger every time she thought about Lassiter. They could have had so much together. One afternoon she took a ride to get away from the house when Ormsby was napping. She ran into Joe Tarsh out near the creek. He came across the plank bridge, grinning. She was certain their meeting was no accident.

"Been keepin' an eye open for you, Claire."

"You know better than to be on this ranch," she snapped.

"I hear Ormsby don't hardly stir outa the house no more."

"Where'd you hear that?"

"Your crew. All two of 'em." He laughed.

On this summer afternoon it didn't take a reading of tea leaves to figure out what Tarsh was after. She still didn't trust him, but on this day she felt a definite need.

It was a hectic reunion with the big handsome ex-foreman with his pale hair, brows and mustache. But nothing to compare with the one when Lassiter had come back with the cattle money. Afterward she smoothed her clothing and sat on the grass, watching the sun play on the stream that was overflow from the lake Ormsby referred to as his bayou. It flowed south for a mile or so and then vanished into an underground channel.

Tarsh rolled a cigarette. "If you're waitin' for Lassiter to come back, forget it. I hear Mexicans 'dobewalled him two weeks ago."

Claire turned cold. Then she glanced at Tarsh's pale eyes under cornsilk brows and she knew he lied. "That so?" she said casually.

"You don't act like you give much of a damn."

"You know the old saying about being out of sight and out of mind."

Tarsh spoke of the ranch she would inherit from Ormsby. "We'll restock it. We'll have us a real spread."

"Restock it with what?"

"Mex cows. I can bring up a thousand head a month till we get all we want."

"That would be risky."

"Mebby," he drawled. Leaning over, he kissed her. It warmed her again. Tarsh said, "I figure the old man's got money buried around this ranch somewheres." He waited a moment, then added slyly, "Either that, or he stumbled onto that Redgate gold."

Suddenly she blurted out the story of Harry Benbow and the black-butted Remington Ormsby had forgotten to return to his safe. "If you hold it just right you can make out a name through that black paint. Colonel Redgate."

Tarsh leaned on an elbow, watching her. "You're makin' this up. You bought one of them damned Redgate treasure maps."

She told him the rest of it. About the detective who couldn't tolerate whiskey without being numbed in body and brain. "He peddled it down at Belleville for a bottle."

"I'll get it back," Tarsh vowed. "I know Dan Rambert, the stuck up sonofabitch. Used to be a professor back East, so they claim. But he shot up half the college over a woman an' come out here to hide. I hear they're still lookin' for him. He gets fancy with me, he'll wish he hadn't."

"Just get the gun," she urged. "Take it apart. There must be a clue." She pressed her mouth against his, fought with her tongue, then drew back, panting. "I'm trusting you, Joe. Remember that."

He nodded. "You figure Ormsby knew Redgate?"

"It's possible."

Tarsh did visit Belleville, saw Dan Rambert's fresh scars on an otherwise presentable face, and listened to him curse Lassiter. He claimed Lassiter had paid fifty dollars for the Redgate gun. And as for Harry Benbow, the detective had died of acute alcoholism, so it was whispered.

In his frustration, Tarsh knocked Rambert down. He strode from Rambert's establishment while Mollie and Ginger squealed in dismay and tried to pick their employer up from the floor and get him to a chair.

"I shall treat him as Hector before the walls of Troy," Rambert muttered through cut lips, "and his blood shall be on the sand."

The two girls didn't know what he was talking about. Later that week when Tarsh got into trouble, it was whispered that Rambert was behind it.

Leland Ormsby knew that this was the day. During the night the old bullet had moved again in his chest. Or at least the pain and pressure from the area of the Civil War wound gave him that impression. Any rational man, even one as old as Ormsby, would have traveled over the mountains to visit a doctor. But Ormsby had always known when his time would come; it was preordained. And it was here!

Over the years he had prepared for his departure. At the edge of the Furnace was his pyramid where he would travel to the next life as a modern pharaoh. He had stumbled on it when first exploring the country that surrounded his ranch. Several people had helped him prepare his sepulcher; all of them were now dead.

Yesterday when Mike Barlow brought the mail out from Tres Vidas, there was a letter from Ormsby's grandson. "Dear Grandfather: This is to let you know that Diana and I are on our way west. I do appreciate the quit claim deed to the ranch and will abide by your stipulation that I change my name. My wife is enjoying our trip and looking forward to meeting you. I know you will be pleased that we hope to walk the same paths you did in your early days in the West. And that includes Virginia City where Father said you were so well known."

Ormsby flew into a rage. "The young fool! Virginia City, of all places!" It was the stress brought on by his fool of a grandson possibly digging into the past that had caused his attack during the night.

Ormsby leaned out a window and yelled at his two ranch hands to hitch up the buckboard. He would drive; they were to ride as escort. They stared at the old man who had shrunk to bones and withered flesh, then hurried to obey his orders.

Claire returned home just as the buckboard was made ready. Ormsby faced her in the parlor. "You are a disappointment to me, Claire." The rigid control he had imposed on diction over the years had slipped away. Today his accent was so thick she could hardly make out what he was saying.

She said stiffly, chin lifted, "I was visiting Mrs. Peterson in Tres Vidas."

"Sleeping with some man in the hotel, you mean."

"Leland, you look awful. Let me put you to bed "

"Ah intended to take you with me on mah final journey. But now you may stay here an' greet mah guests."

Her green eyes were questioning. "What guests?"

"Tell him when he comes that—" Ormsby winced and sank to one of the heavy Spanish chairs. He pressed a fist against his chest, fighting for breath. Then he began to mutter and she had to lean close in order to try and make out what he was saying over and over. It sounded like, "Tell him . . . buy your gold, buy your gold . . ."

Ormsby's color seemed suddenly better. He looked up at out of bright, malicious eyes. And he was grinning in that satanic way of his. "Tell him what ah said. Tell that young man . . ." He broke off and struggled out of the chair. She tried to help him but he twisted away.

"Tell him what, Leland? Buy your gold? That's the way it sounded to me. And what young man are you talking about?"

"Mah grandson." And he told her the rest of it and enjoyed watching the color slowly leave her handsome face. "But don't look so downcast, mah dear," he consoled, patting her on the arm. "With your charms you can take him away from his wife. You may wind up owning the ranch after all."

She stood stunned, unbelieving.

"Ah feel that ah am about to depart on a rather unusual journey," he said.

"I hope not," she said. "You'll be around for a long time. Surely you were joshing me about leaving the ranch to your grandson."

"Ah did not josh."

"But you told me you had no relatives!" Rage was starting to steam through her again. "You said you were alone in the world."

"Ah know ah said that."

"The ranch was supposed to be mine!" she shouted at the emaciated husk of human confronting her.

"Frankly, ah am surprised at you, Claire, to believe what a man tells you in bed." He chuckled, a whisper of sound from the withered throat. "Ah decided months ago to burden mah grandson with this ranch."

"After all I've done for you!"

"Your flesh has warmed mine and that is the extent of it, mah dear."

"You know I did everything you asked."

"And when you left mah bed, you went to other men."

"I'm young and hot-blooded, but you know that. You—"

Bones were prominent in the hand that waved her to silence. "Farewell, Claire." He drew her hand to his lips. She was revolted. He let her hand fall and left the house.

She was still numbed when she saw him, from a window, go rattling out of the ranchyard in the buckboard, looking like a gnome as he drove the team, reins tightly wrapped around his skeletal hands. Barlow and Canfield rode their horses into the wagon dust. Claire went to the office and tried to find evidence of the grandson. But the stove was filled with ash and she knew he had burned everything.

Flinging herself into Ormsby's big chair, she tried to think. She eyed the ominous weapon beneath the desk and wondered how many lives it had taken. How many corpses were rotting in secret graves? What she needed was a smart man to help her. But who? Tarsh was down on the border and Lassiter. . . . A half-dozen times a day his image strode across her mind. She would silently curse that image and then in the next breath smother it with endearments. Noticing a spider at work at a comer of the ceiling made up her mind for her. She would spin her own web as she waited for Ormsby's grandson to arrive. It wouldn't be the first time she had stolen a husband away from a wife. With any luck, she still might be mistress of OS ranch.

Ormsby's arms felt as if weighted with chains and he had difficulty getting his breath. But the familiar satanic grin was still on the wrinkled lips. Driving the buckboard to Tres Vidas had tired him more than he thought possible. If he had any doubt that his life was hurtling inexorably to its conclusion, they were soon stilled.

Emilio Ruiz commented on Ormsby's rare visit to his cantina. Ormsby said he had some cattle to move with his two ranch hands. Barlow and Canfield had one drink and then went outside to wait. Ormsby slumped at a table and when he had caught his breath, bought a bottle of whiskey from Ruiz which the saloonman placed in a gunnysack for him.

"You drink whiskey and your vaqueros do the work, eh?" Ruiz chuckled and handed him the sack.

"Put it on the ranch bill, Emilio."

"Of course, senor." Ormsby's Spanish was so laced with Southern accent that Ruiz had trouble understanding him.

"Ah wonder if there is a paymaster in hell. If so, present the bill to him."

"You are very pale, senor. Pale as death."

"Ah will be shaking his hand. Mah journey begins soon "

Ormsby was about to hoist himself onto his spindly legs when the doors popped open. Joe Tarsh, big and blond and belligerent, stalked in.

"Just the man ah need," Ormsby said with a cackling laugh. "Ah want you to come back to work for me."

Sound of his former employer's voice brought Tarsh's head whipping around.

"Kind of sudden you wantin' me back," Tarsh said warily. He had just disposed of nearly a thousand head of cattle across the line. His buyer had not been particular about unhealed brands that had been recently altered.

The only reason Tarsh even considered taking on his old job again was the availability of Claire. Ormsby looked to be about at the end of his tether. A strong breath would blow him right off the chair. When Ormsby was six feet under, Claire would own the ranch. Stock it with rustled beef, the brands worked over with a running iron, and he and Claire would be heading for the stars.

"Had ah known where to reach you, mah boy, ah would have gotten in touch with you long ago."

Tarsh decided to go along with it. What the hell, there was nothing to lose.

Ruiz watched them leave the cantina together. He was to remember the scene when relating it later to Sheriff Joplin.

"Got something ah want to show you, Joe," Ormsby said as Tarsh helped him into the buckboard. "Somethin' that's been hidden for a long time."

Tarsh's throat tightened and the palms of his hands grew moist as he considered the possibilities. What Claire had said about Redgate gold crossed his mind.

Tarsh drove the buckboard, one of the ranch hands leading the saddler. Barlow and Canfield wondered if they would still have jobs now that the old foreman seemed to be back in Ormsby's favor. They had been in Tres Vidas the day Lassiter had humiliated Tarsh by taking away his gun. Today Tarsh had given them cold nods. Their only hope was the fact that old man Ormsby seemed to like them. He mentioned a good bonus for the work they were to do for him today.

They had no idea what he had in mind, but they did begin to get a little nervous when Tarsh wheeled the buckboard off the only decent road across the Furnace and began following a set of dim wheel tracks through cactus and sand dunes. And with Ormsby gesturing and giving him directions in his shrill old man's voice.

Tarsh noticed that the jolting of the wagon finally jarred some items loose from under the seat. Rattling onto the floorboards was a saber covered with a thick coat of black paint and a Remington revolver. Its butt was painted black. Tarsh remembered what Claire had told him. Either it was the gun the detective had pawned at Belleville or a mate. There was also a .30-30 Winchester on the floorboards, this weapon with an ordinary walnut stock and unpainted.

Tarsh let the old man ramble, which he had been doing most of the way. Occasionally he would break off to peer with dimming eyesight at hills and rock formations. Looking for landmarks, he told Tarsh. Then he would resume talking of ancient Egypt and pharaohs who knew how to leave the world and be prepared for the next. Tarsh was vaguely aware that there was such a place as Egypt, but the rest of it made no sense.

"This pharaoh hombre you're talkin' about, Ormsby, is he an ancestor of yours?" Tarsh asked just to keep the old man happy.

"Ah am the pharaoh." Ormsby chuckled. "And by the way, the name is not Ormsby, but Redgate."

Torah felt a sudden cold prickly sensation down his backbone. As one of the primitives of the world, Tarsh had an instinctive fear of the insane.

Tarsh thought about it, wondered if Ormsby was making a joke, then said, "You the fella makes them Redgate maps?" Tarsh laughed but it caught in his throat when he saw a benign smile on the mouth that reminded him of a knife slit in a withered apple.

"No, but a man tried to sell me such a map once," Ormsby said. "It was years ago when Tres Vidas was only a way station. This man insisted the map was genuine." Ormsby's bleat of wild laughter dried Tarsh's mouth. He edged away as far as possible on the seat of the swaying buckboard.

"Ah am the only one in the world who knows where the gold is hidden," Ormsby said. "Why should ah need a map? Is that not right, Joe? Why should ah need a map?"

"You told this to the hombre tryin' to sell you the map?" Tarsh probed.

"Of course not, Joe. At that time ah had no intention of revealing mah true identity."

"That you're really Colonel Redgate."

"At your service, suh."

"Jesus Christ!"

"Ah have surprised you, Joe." Ormsby's chuckles sounded to Tarsh like the rattle of dry bones in a barrel.

"Where the hell are we going, anyhow?" Tarsh demanded, slowing the team. Dust boiled behind them, covering the pair of riders in their wake.

"Patience, Joe," Ormsby counseled. "Patience. Ah need a strong man and the gods have sent me you. Ah had counted on Lassiter—"

"Don't mention that bastard."

"He proved a disappointment. Ah groomed Claire to accompany me also, but she proved to be treacherous."

"But she'll inherit your ranch, huh?"

"The meek shall inherit the earth, Joe. But we will be far from this sphere of mud hurtling through space. We will not need the likes of Claire, mah boy.

We will have all the women we desire. Gold will buy even more in the next world than this."

Tarsh could make out only about half of what the old man was saying because Ormsby's tongue seemed thick and there was the bang and rattle of the wagon.

The only thing that kept Tarsh from turning back was a weird feeling that maybe, just maybe, Ormsby had stumbled onto the Redgate gold and was leading him to it. Why else would they be crossing the bleakest part of a moonscape known as the Furnace?

They came at last to a rocky hillside half hidden by detritus and rocks the size of melons. There was also a scattering of giant boulders.

Tarsh pulled up at Ormsby's command. The team stood, heads down, tails and manes blowing in the faint breeze that had sprung up in the last mile or so.

Ormsby issued instructions to the two ranch hands. Barlow, graying and nervous, looked apprehensively at the hillside. Canfield lifted a hat from his bald head, scratched his pate. Both middle-aged riders exchanged glances. Barlow made a circular motion with a forefinger at his temple when Ormsby was looking the other way.

"Perform well for me today and you will never want," the old man was saying. "Either in this life or the next. Ah will see to that."

Both men pulled on heavy work gloves the boss had ordered them to bring. They followed his instructions and went to work, throwing rocks aside from the spot Ormsby had designated. Tarsh stood beside the wagon as Ormsby strode up and down, elaborating on his orders and sounding like an overseer.

"Just what the hell is this s'posed to mean?" Tarsh finally asked after he had stood silent for nearly half an hour.

Ormsby waved a bony hand at the opening in the hillside that an industrious Barlow and Canfield were gradually enlarging. "The gateway to paradise," Ormsby informed him with a smile that revealed his bad teeth.

"Gateway to paradise?" Tarsh listened to the thud of rocks which the ranch hands plucked from the opening in the hillside and then tossed into a growing pile. Tarsh felt a chill. He looked over his shoulder at the wheel tracks the wagon had left in the sand. Already they were being partially covered by sand in the growing wind. Out on the vast expanse of desert he could see no sign of movement, either animal or human.

Ormsby said, "As the pharaohs chose their pyramids, ah chose mine, at this site. You recall the expert with that newfangled dynamite an' his assistant?"

Tarsh studied the parchment-like profile. "Sure I remember," he said carefully, wondering what wheels were spinning wildly inside the shrunken skull.

"You were busy with roundup so ah stayed out here with mah two friends. Until the work was completed. An' a fine job they did, Joe. A fine job."

"Them are the two you said you catched tryin' to bust into your safe," Tarsh reminded.

"That ah did, suh. An' when they thought ah was just a helpless old man, they grew careless. An' I taunted 'em into leanin' over mah desk. Two birds with one shot. Ah got 'em both, didn't ah, Joe?"

"Well, yeah."

"You buried the two would-be robbers. Remember, Joe?" Ormsby chuckled as if the episode with the dynamite expert and assistant was one huge joke.

Tarsh's uneasiness became a burgeoning fear. Was the old bastard in some way going to try and blame him for the murders? There had been more than those two gunned down by the hidden weapon so hair-trigger that only the touch of a boot toe would set it off. The only inconvenience to such a system was periodic replacement of the desk top.

By now the hole in the side of the hill was large enough so a man could walk through upright. Tarsh saw that the rocks the two sweating ranch hands were removing had cleverly masked the opening of a cave.

Tarsh suddenly turned on Ormsby. "I don't want no more of this!"

Ormsby looked stricken as he vaulted into the saddle. "But ah want you with me, Joe. Ah need you."

"Go to hell. You're *loco en la cabeza* for sure." Tarsh spurred away.

Barlow and Canfield, faces stained with dust and perspiration, knew enough Spanish to recognize the shouted description of their employer's mental status. Ormsby coaxed the pair back to work. They exchanged glances, shrugged. Barlow said in a low voice, "My guess is that there's money inside that cave." Canfield silently agreed.

But as they continued work, Canfield got to thinking about it. "The old man looks about done in. He dies, an' they claim we done him in, we could end up in the Fortress."

Barlow shivered. "Christ, don't talk like that. Let's finish the job so's he can pay us an' we'll be gone."

Ormsby said he wanted the opening large enough to accommodate the buckboard. "The pharaoh always had a boat to take him over the horizon. Ah will use a wagon."

They didn't hear him because the rocks they were hurling aside with renewed energy made a great clatter and thump.

Finally Ormsby entered the cave, looking pleased. Floor, ceiling and walls were solid rock, save for a very narrow natural vent in the ceiling. A niche had been cut in the side walls. Each niche held a candle. Ormsby scratched a match and lit first one candle then the other.

In the center of the cave, resting on slabs of rock, was a hardwood coffin. Daylight from the opening touched it for the first time. Barlow's jaw dropped. Canfield stood as if transfixed.

Ormsby ordered them to unhitch the team from the wagon. "Then wheel it in here, boys," Ormsby said happily. "An' then your earthly chores will be finished."

Because of the narrow opening, the wheel hubs on the wagon scraped rock and got hung up. Desperately the two men shoved and pulled until they got it into the cave. It bumped against the coffin.

"Careful, boys," Ormsby cautioned them.

They watched him removing items from the buckboard. A long sword painted black. And an oversize revolver, the butt coated with the same black paint. It looked like a big Remington. Ormsby, breathing hard, placed these in the coffin.

"Mah golden saber, mah golden gun," he wheezed. "Whoever stole mah other gun, I consign to hellfire."

The last two items Ormsby placed in the coffin were a Winchester and the quart of whiskey. Then as Barlow and Canfield looked on fearfully, the old man clambered into the coffin, gasping for breath. His face was ashen when he seated himself in the coffin, uncorked the bottle of whiskey and took a long gurgling drink.

"Come closer, boys," he said weakly, lowering the bottle. "An' ah will reward you for your efforts on mah behalf."

Barlow had turned to stare out the cave mouth where a dust storm was beginning to thicken. By that time he couldn't even see the wagon team. Had the old fool cut them loose while they were working? Or had they been spooked by the sudden blast of wind and sand? He couldn't move. It was as if he were chained to the stone floor.

When Ormsby beckoned again, Canfield said hoarsely, "What the hell do you want from us?"

"To reward you, mah faithful slaves."

Barlow suddenly found his voice and was screaming to Canfield about the horses he could no longer see.

"Mebbe we're afoot!"

But Canfield could barely hear him above the howl of the storm. Sand shushed into the opening in a choking cloud.

Barlow seized his friend by an arm, trying to get him to move. But Canfield seemed in a trance. However, he came out of it when he saw Ormsby lift the rife and was convinced the old man intended to murder them both.

"Run!" the panic-stricken Canfield shouted. Barlow was already moving. They both pounded past the buckboard and plunged headlong toward the opening in the hillside.

Barlow, with a head start, actually reached the opening and was halfway through when Ormsby aimed the rifle, centering it not on the fleeing men but at a bull's eye in white paint on the south cave wall and to one side of the rubble that filled part of the entrance. A sharp report from the rifle was nothing compared to the sudden roar that seemed to lift the earth itself. Canfield screamed as an avalanche of rock poured down to seal off the entrance. But the dynamite and caps, to be set off with a rifle bullet, had been so skillfully placed that the rear of the cave was only jolted.

Although the air was filled with dust and fumes from the dynamite, Ormsby survived the blast. And within seconds the air began to clear, the fumes drawn up through the natural vent in the cave roof. One of the candles went out. In the flickering light of the remaining candle, Ormsby tilted the bottle for another drink. Suddenly the reserve strength that had kept him going for most of that pain-filled afternoon finally drained away. He fell back into the coffin, a husk of corpse.

The only sound left in the sepulcher was that of the whiskey bottle that had slipped from his hand to shatter on the stone floor.

Chapter Nine

Although there were some, including Sheriff Joplin, who were reasonably certain that Joe Tarsh had murdered Leland Ormsby, no body was found. The old man had simply disappeared. So it was ironical to many residents of the sparsely settled area that Tarsh was arrested not for murder but for rustling.

His one hope, after being locked up in the Fortress, was Claire Manning.

It was a full day when Claire, wearing black, which she assumed to be proper attire for a prison, visited Tarsh at the Fortress. In the roofless visitor's room, used whenever weather permitted, she was chilled by sight of a Gatling gun trained on the table where she waited for Tarsh. It was in a tower on the prison wall and manned by two uniformed guards.

Tarsh appeared through a barred door which was slammed and locked. The clanging of metal dried Claire's mouth, for the sound was an ominous reminder that here some men were imprisoned for what Judge Garvenoo termed "the rest of your natural life." Claire knew of a woman doing forty years in Yuma Prison. So being female was no bar to stone walls and endless punishment. The Fortress, even more infamous than Yuma, was known to foster suicides and escapes. Suicides were free, but escapes came dear. It was whispered that a cattleman had given up his ranch in exchange for his son's escape. Both were now living in France. A mine owner was said to have paid thirty thousand dollars to rescue a brother from the Fortress. No one seemed quite sure just how the escapes were managed. But it was no secret that they cost a lot of money in this corrupt southern half of the territory, most of it going to the prison superintendent and his brother-in-law, captain of the guards.

"Thank God you managed it, Claire," Tarsh said hoarsely, sinking to a bench across from her.

She arched her brows. "I wore a tight dress."

He ran an appreciative eye over the black silk.

"Yeah," he breathed. "Fits like skin. What I'd give to peel it."

"Your letter said it was urgent that I see you."

"Sure is. Didn't know whether you'd come or not."

"Maybe I need some answers." She looked carefully around. The two guards in the tower leaned against the Gatling gun with its polished brass and multiple barrels. Another guard with a rifle scowled at her through the barred door to the visitor's room. She had been warned not to touch the prisoner, nor even lean across the table that separated them. Tarsh would be severely punished if she did.

"What happened the day Leland disappeared?" she asked, her voice tight with anxiety.

"Never mind that," Tarsh snapped. But he wore a smile so that anyone would assume the mood was carefree, that they weren't grimly plotting something. But Tarsh was. He said that he wanted her to find some way to get in touch with Lassiter. That surprised her so much that she lost the smile Tarsh had instructed her to wear throughout their meeting.

"But you *hate* Lassiter," she reminded.

"For money, I don't hate. *One million dollars*!" He said it so she read his lips.

She was wary. Although Tarsh had only been in the Fortress a short time it had already thinned him down, a wildness in his hard blue eyes. Had it affected his mind?

He also mouthed, "Get hold of Lassiter."

"But I don't know where he is."

"He hangs out at the Eagle Hotel in El Paso. A letter oughta reach him."

"What in the world am I supposed to tell him about *the million dollars*?" The last of it she had mouthed as he had done.

Tarsh threw back his head and laughed as if she had said something that amused him. But his voice was tense as he said softly, "I know where Ormsby hid his money."

"Ormsby has disappeared. They think he's dead, but there's no body."

"I know where it is," he said softly. "He's buried with his money. I heard a hell of a blast. I figured out how he did it. But before I could go back and look, a posse grabbed me. They were after me for a job I did on some cows with a runnin' iron. It was after I was put in here that I figured out the rest of it."

"Tell me," she asked tensely.

"The old man figured to have me buried with him. And you too."

"Me?"

"Don't look so grim. Smile, smile. Yeah, the old man wanted company. Somethin' about an afterlife. He likely got it with Canfield. An' I hear that Barlow's out of it."

She studied Tarsh again, more carefully, to see if she could detect madness. She had seen it in poor Mike Barlow; his friend Canfield had disappeared the same day as Ormsby. Barlow had finally wandered into Tres Vidas on foot. He would sit all day on the loafer's bench and stare into space. His graying hair had turned white. Nobody could get anything out of him. Aggie Simms at the store fed him and gave him a blanket and a shed to sleep in. There was speculation that his sidekick Canfield might have killed Ormsby and hidden the body. Others thought Joe Tarsh had been in on it. Tarsh had been seen leaving Tres Vidas in a wagon with Ormsby and the two ranch hands. Ormsby and Canfield were never seen again. And Tarsh had been arrested for rustling that same day. And Barlow hadn't uttered a word since. He seemed harmless but there was talk of sending him north to the mad house at Trixton Meadows to spend the rest of his life chained to a wall with the other inmates.

Tarsh still had that grin pasted to his lips, but his voice was harsh. "Get hold of Lassiter. That bastard'll do anything for money."

"Just like you, Joe," she reminded.

"And I can trust him. He brought back the old man's cattle money." He elaborated on his plans. "Tell Lassiter to pretend he's from a newspaper and wants to write about me stealin' cows on both sides of the line."

"You've already got fifteen years to do here," she reminded him, smiling for the guard. "You start bragging and they might add on a few more."

"Just do what I ask. Tell Lassiter to use the name of Alcorn. Ben Alcorn. Was a cousin of mine."

"Just what does Lassiter get out of all this."

"Me an' him split Ormsby's money."

"If Ormsby's dead, he died broke. I should know."

"Ormsby and Colonel Redgate were one and the same." Tarsh looked triumphant. "And he's buried with that missing gold."

"That's all a myth," she said with a straight face.

"The hell it is." Tarsh's eyes were shining and he seemed almost buoyant, the Tarsh she remembered. The handsome one, not the haggard prisoner who had lost ten pounds or more and had a haunted look about him. But talk of money had transformed his face. She had always had a weakness for the handsome no-good ones: Tarsh and Harry Benbow. And Lassiter. He might be a little better than the others but he was still a bastard.

"I'll tell Lassiter where the money is," Tarsh said. "He can buy me outa this place. Then it's you an' me for South America. You'll live like a duchess."

"What makes you think Lassiter can get in here as a reporter?" she wanted to know.

"One was already here last week. From a newspaper in Nevada. Virginia City, I think it was. Ryan was a good talker."

"Ryan?"

She didn't tell Tarsh that a newspaperman named Ryan had showed up at the ranch. She also didn't tell him that Ormsby's grandson and wife were living there. For the first time since trying to tell Lassiter about the Redgate gold, she had a feeling she might end up rich after all. If Tarsh really knew where the money was buried, that is. And she did believe he wasn't lying. Not about that, at least. Not if he hoped to use part of it to buy his way out of this hellhole.

She stood up when the guard signaled that the visiting time was over. She smiled at Tarsh and walked out, her body swaying provocatively in the expensive black silk that Ormsby had bought for her from a catalogue. Word was passed and every guard in the place managed to be near the front gate to witness her departure.

Captain of the Guard Beeler strutted up, took her arm, and walked her through the gate. "If Tarsh showed me a thousand in gold," he said with a leer, "I'd let you spend the night. And when he was finished you could have the next one with me. At no cost."

Instead of a caustic rejoinder, she smiled and walked to the wagon where she was to be driven to the ranch by Bruce Redgate.

"Did you learn anything?" he asked eagerly, when he was driving the team down the steep road.

"Nothing." She made herself sound despondent.

"I was so hoping you'd learn what happened to my grandfather. And his money."

She only shrugged. She might have confided in him to a point, had it not been for that simpering pale-haired wife of his. Men had a habit of talking too much when they were in bed. Whether it was his wife, mistress, or casual woman.

Bruce had talked to Claire, in fact told her everything that first night after his wife retired early, worn out from the long stagecoach ride from Santa Rita.

All the way back to the ranch Claire framed the letter she would write to Lassiter. Somehow she had to make him believe her. Whether he would or not was another matter. One thing for sure, if things worked out as she hoped they would, she'd be Lassiter's duchess in South America, not Tarsh's. She spent most of her night composing her letter until she got it just right.

Time dragged much worse in the Fortress than in the numerous jails Tarsh had been in at one time or another. He was given the worst jobs in the prison. He went without sleep because he spent most of the days mopping the many corridors and half the nights working in the kitchen. He grew jumpy because he had heard nothing from Lassiter, nor had Claire tried to see him again to report.

It was on a particularly rugged day that Tarsh had a doubled rope-end, first soaked in a tub of salt water, laid ten times across his bared back because of a minor infraction of the rules. Captain Beeler wielded the rope.

In the painful aftermath, he reviewed his position. Either Claire had failed to get in touch with Lassiter, or Lassiter had ignored her plea. No matter which way it had gone, Tarsh knew that if he was to survive he had to rely on no one but himself.

It was time for the conference that Captain of the Guards Beeler had been hinting at for so long.

Some days later Tarsh was transferred to a wing of the prison that was seldom used. There were six cells, only one of them occupied and this by an American, Deacon Hipp, who had terrorized Mexico for a time. He had fled to the U.S. side of the border, been involved in shooting, had tried to reach his friend Dan Rambert at Belleville but was grabbed by Sheriff Joplin.

Tarsh was locked in one of the cells. The door was of iron bars. An outer door of planks bolted together could be swung into place. A barred window overlooked the prison wall twenty feet away. When Beeler and two guards had departed, Tarsh went to the door. By pressing his face to the bars Tarsh could barely make out the other occupant of the prison wing. Deacon Hipp had been trying to get his attention.

"Bringin' you back here they must figure to let you bust out," Hipp said when they had introduced themselves.

Tarsh made no comment. He spoke of the beating with the rope-end. The lacerated back still bothered him. Since the whipping he had been in the "hole." It was good to see daylight again.

"What you in for?" Hipp called to him.

"Usin' a runnin' iron."

Hipp laughed. "Stealing cows don't make you rich."

"Keep at it long enough it will."

"If you don't get caught."

Tarsh said nothing to that. Beeler had promised to have a talk with someone higher up. Tarsh knew it was Beeler's brother-in-law, superintendent of the prison. "What'd they throw you in here for?" Tarsh wanted to know.

"Got away with a payroll. Silver mine owned by Americans. Mine guards killed everybody but me. I hid out in the Sierra Madres with my woman. She brings in ten thousand dollars at a time. I got ten thousand to go, an' then I get to bust my ass outa this place."

Tarsh had no intention of revealing his own plans. "Good luck!" he called out.

Then he went to his cot and laid down. Beeler had given him an extra strong dose of laudanum to ease the pain of the healing lacerations on his back. Beeler was so concerned all of a sudden with Tarsh's health. Tarsh wanted to laugh, but he hurt too much to try. Until things worked out, he would live well. No more mops, no more kitchen work.

The worst part about it all was that he had to trust Beeler. And Beeler's brother-in-law, Silas Tighe, who ran the damned prison. He would rather have trusted Lassiter. But he had no choice. Otherwise he would die in this place. Beeler had hinted at the possibility often enough.

Chapter Ten

Lassiter faced a distraught, green-eyed Claire Manning. It was on the veranda of the ranch house where he had come that day weeks ago with the money satchel, tired and dusty and nearly out on his feet. Today on crossing the Furnace the air had been mild, the sky clear.

"You can't go back, Claire," Lassiter told her. "Even blink your eye and you can't unblink it. The only time that counts is now."

"But if you had only believed in me."

"To hell with what's happened in the past." It was after further futile attempts to bolster the fortunes of Dona Esperanza, the beautiful dark-eyed widow of his compadre Don Benito, that Lassiter read an item in an El Paso paper: the sudden disappearance of Leland Ormsby, prominent rancher. It started Lassiter thinking again about the Redgate gold.

A long shot, sure, as had been everything else Lassiter had tried during the past year. It was time for a break in his streak of back luck.

Claire spoke of the grandson who was living in the house with his young wife. "The kid's name is Redgate."

"Things are adding up," Lassiter said softly. He suggested they get away from the house so they couldn't be overheard.

As they walked to the lake, Claire said, "You didn't seem surprised about Redgate. It was also Ormsby's real name."

Lassiter halted, gave her a sardonic smile. "Yeah, the old man told me."

"Leland *told* you?" She pushed back her black hair and looked at him in amazement.

"Said he was Colonel Redgate," Lassiter admitted.

"And what did you do then?" she demanded.

"Laughed."

"Oh, you *fool*! He was practically handing it to you."

"That's when he tried to blow me apart with that trick gun."

She leaned against a tree as if the strength had suddenly gone out of her legs. "At least my letter brought you back."

He said he had never received her letter.

"Then why did you come back?" she wanted to know.

"Hunch."

Drawing a deep breath, she said, "Why the devil weren't your hunches working before? Now we've Tarsh to contend with."

He narrowed his eyes. "Tarsh? What's he got to do with it?"

She spoke of Tarsh's troubles with the law, his confinement in the Fortress. "He says he trusts you."

"Yeah, I can imagine," Lassiter said dryly.

She gripped him by the arms, her teeth bared. "Listen to me for a change. If you had listened before, then we wouldn't have to share with Tarsh. And others."

"What others?" he demanded.

When she spoke of the captain of the guards and the prison superintendent, Lassiter realized it was going to be tougher than he had thought at first. And he had to kick himself for having laughed at Ormsby that day. But as he had told Claire, there was no going back.

Claire glanced over her shoulder at the big house that loomed with white walls and red-tiled roof through the screening cottonwoods. "The old man's grandson came just after you had gone away. He claimed his grandfather insisted he change his name to Ormsby. But it looks as if the old man is dead so Bruce is calling himself Redgate."

"Hearing that name will sure stir up the hornets," Lassiter said sourly. "Everybody will be hunting for the gold."

Claire shook her dark head. "I talked Bruce into calling himself Ormsby whenever anybody came by. He said he'd do it as a favor to me. At least for now."

Lassiter looked at her. "The kid trusts you, huh?"

"Hardly anyone has come to the ranch. And I've kept the Redgates from going to Tres Vidas. And the two ranch hands are out of it. Canfield disappeared with the old man. And Barlow is crazy as a loon. Nobody can get anything out of him."

"Main thing is what Tarsh told you about the money," Lassiter said impatiently.

"He didn't tell me a thing."

"Don't try and make me believe that," he scoffed.

"It's true. The only way Tarsh can get out of that corrupt hellhole is to buy his way out. And that means Captain Beeler and his brother-in-law Silas Tighe."

"Then we might as well forget it, Claire."

"You can do it, Lassiter. I know you can. And if we don't move fast, Tarsh could end up dead in that place."

"That wouldn't surprise me from what they say of the Fortress."

She told him of visiting Tarsh at the prison. "Tarsh says you're the only one he knows who can help him."

"I should stick my neck in a bear trap just to help him?"

"But he swears he knows where Leland buried the money."

"I wouldn't take much stock in what Tarsh swears."

"But it's true. A feeling I have."

"He was your lover once. Is that the feeling you've got? Heat?"

"Lassiter, it's the money. Nothing else."

He turned that over in his mind, then said, "Well, how am I supposed to go about it?"

"Get in to see Tarsh. And you'd better hurry. If they find Leland's body, Tarsh is liable to hang for murder."

"Did he admit to you that he killed the old man?"

"Tarsh swears he was alive when he left him."

"Left him where?" Lassiter's dark brows lifted.

"In a cave at the edge of the Furnace. And there isn't time to waste. If Sheriff Joplin finds Leland's body . . ."

"Looks like the sheriff is panting to get his favorite brand of rope justice. But I don't think there's much worry there, come to think of it."

"You don't know Joplin."

"A body won't last in the Furnace. Never has, never will. Predators will get at it one way or another."

"I'd hate to bet my life on it. Sheriff Joplin was out here. He threatened me, but I stood my ground. He's left me alone since then."

Lassiter eyed her cynically, wondering if she had stood her ground by offering herself to the sheriff. More than one lawman had been bribed by a fetching female.

Before he could dwell on that he saw a young couple come storming out of the house to the veranda. The woman was a young blonde in a pink dress, the man only slightly taller wearing a white shirt. His hair was tousled, his face red. There was a lot of armwaving and shrill voices. Because of the distance, Lassiter couldn't make out what was being said.

"Diana and Bruce," Claire said, wrinkling her now.

"They always fight like this?"

"Bruce thinks he's in love with me." Claire shrugged as the young couple returned to the house, slamming the door. "He swears he never had a woman before his marriage."

"And you showed him what he's missed?"

She admitted it. "Now when somebody speaks of bliss, he knows what it means."

Lassiter laughed. "He couldn't have a better teacher. Main thing now is to tell me just how in hell I'm supposed to get in the Fortress and see Tarsh."

"Then you'll do it, Lassiter, you'll play along with us?"

"I'll think about it."

She had to accept that. "At the Fortress you pose as a newspaperman named Ben Alcorn. Say that you're from a newspaper and you want to interview Tarsh."

"This sounds like the dreams that come out of an opium pipe," Lassiter said thinly.

"It'll work, really it will, Lassiter."

"You make it sound easy. How do you know they'll even let me see him?"

He listened to her tell about the newspaperman named Ryan who had already interviewed Tarsh. "Tarsh says this Gil Ryan is somehow connected with the Empire Mine that Colonel Redgate got all that gold bullion from."

"How much did Tarsh tell him?"

"He swears not a thing. Ryan tried, but couldn't get anything out of him. Oh, Lassiter, it'll mean so much to us."

He read the promise in the green eyes and said, "I've got time for a quick reunion at the far side of the lake." He gestured at the thick trees near their favorite plot of grass. But Claire stepped back and shook her head.

"I promised Bruce I'd be faithful."

"You trying to make me laugh?"

"He's very serious about such things," she said with a straight face.

"He's got a wife in one part of the house and you in a spare bedroom and he worries about you being faithful?"

"He does. And listen to something else, Lassiter. If this works out—the money I mean—I'm yours. For all time. But until then I've got a right to have a spare ace in my hand."

"You mean take him away from his wife and marry the ranch?"

"Exactly. Maybe it sounds cruel, but I've got to look out for myself." Tears started at her eyes, glistening in the sun. "Damn it, if you'd only listened to me before we wouldn't have to—"

Lassiter knuckled her chin, forcing her to meet his eyes. "I don't give a damn what you do with Bruce, or anybody. All I'm going to think about now is the money."

Her eyes were shining when she said, "And when we've got our share of the money I'll give you a reception you'll never forget."

Chapter Eleven

In a village across the border lived a man who periodically fashioned "ancient" treasure maps and other documents as well. His talents were appreciated on both sides of the line.

Lassiter mentioned Alejandro Abran, the blind guitaron player of Belleville, who was a relative.

"Mi primo," said the man. They were in his living quarters in the company of three growling dogs nearly as old and toothless as this cousin of Abran's. He was a short and round little man with wiry gray hair.

Lassiter explained what he wanted. "Proof that I am a journalist with the name Ben Alcorn." The old man wrote it down, then waddled over to a heavy door. He unlocked it and beckoned for Lassiter to follow him. The room was cramped with tables and shelves that contained many official-looking papers.

The old man named a price for his services, two hundred dollars. Lassiter said the job had to be done that day. That would cost an extra hundred dollars. Lassiter agreed.

He spent the day sipping mescal in a nearby cantina. Several girls with dark hair and shining eyes tried to get his attention. For one of the few times in his life he was uninterested. The long chance of getting his hands on a fortune in gold bullion demanded all of his attention. He knew there could be no slip-ups in the hazardous game he had elected to play. And if he did get to see Tarsh, what then? He and the ex-foreman had been far from friendly, but this was a joint venture that demanded they bury the hatchet. And hopefully not in each other's heads. If he could reach Tarsh, he would have word of the money, according to Claire, and go on from there. He intended to play the game straight if others did likewise. But if Tarsh or anyone else tried to play fancy, then all bets were off.

Abran's cousin was a genius, no doubt about that, Lassiter decided as he scanned an identification card proclaiming him to be Ben Alcorn. And with it was a letter from the editor of the El Paso Sentinel assigning this Ben Alcorn to get an interview with a prisoner named Joe Tarsh. The subject: rustling, and how existing laws could be tightened so as to protect the cattleman from further thefts.

Lassiter paid the old man and said, "With your talents you should sit at the right hand of El Presidente." Lassiter complimented him in Spanish for a remarkable job well done. Working with a broken-down old press, doing all the hand lettering in the back room of a ramshackle adobe in a border village that was little more than a flyspeck on the map of Mexico.

The old man smiled around a cornhusk cigarette pasted to a lower lip. "It is safer here than at the right hand of El Presidente," he said slyly. "Porfirio Diaz and I do not agree on many things."

Lassiter had to risk further delay because he needed to dress like a newspaperman and his decent clothing was in El Paso. He couldn't masquerade as a journalist and be dressed as a range bum. If he intended to play with rattlesnakes the odds had to be whittled as much as possible.

He located three Anglos who had a wagonload of clothing, some of it slightly used, most of it new. Nothing new fit him. He bought a dark suit, a white shirt and string tie. No doubt the merchandise had come from a frontier store, from houses in the more fashionable districts of town. A risky venture for such a paltry retum. Lassiter played for the big return or not at all.

As he rode north in his tight suit, he experienced his first apprehension upon seeing the Fortress in the distance, looming like a medieval fortification on the brow of a row of hills. It was whispered that the few desperate men who had made it over the walls, were soon cut to pieces by Gatling guns. The superintendent, Silas Tighe, had often bragged that no one ever escaped in the five years the prison had been in operation. But it was also known that escapes could be managed, for a price.

Lassiter tied his horse to a rack and presented the forged credentials to a guard with a shotgun. The man's small and suspicious eyes roved over Lassiter.

"Tarsh is gettin' famous all of a sudden," the guard grumbled. "Another fella come to see him recent."

Lassiter wondered about it, said innocently, "A relative?"

"Newspaperman."

"Competition, eh?" Lassiter drawled, but he got the information he wanted.

"Newspaperman from Nevada. Second time he come here. This time Tarsh wouldn't see him. Likely you won't have no better luck, Alcorn."

Lassiter looked blank for a moment, then remembered he was supposed to be Ben Alcorn.

The guard said, "You'll have to wait till I go see Roy Beeler. Here he comes now."

A stocky man in a gray suit was shown Lassiter's credentials. "Want I should send him away?" the guard asked.

Beeler smiled at Lassiter. "Welcome, Mr. Alcorn." He handed back the letter and the card. "Step right inside."

Something about the man's smile made Lassiter suspicious. Beeler had a shaved bull neck. A thick mustache hid the corners of his too-generous smile.

Warning signals buzzed in Lassiter's skull as Beeler stepped aside so he could enter the narrow slot where the heavy gate was partially open. "The guard here claims Tarsh refused to see another newspaperman."

"He'll see you," Beeler said, losing a little of the welcoming smile. Beeler's voice had acquired an edge that the guard caught; he shifted the shotgun so that it covered Lassiter. And Beeler had hooked a thumb in a shellbelt above a holstered .45.

"Step inside, Mr. Alcorn," Beeler said.

Lassiter knew that if he tried to back off now that shotgun could cut him in two. He broadened his smile and said, "Thanks for making it easy for me, Mr. Beeler." And he stepped through the gate. It was slammed shut at his back and locked.

In the superintendent's office Lassiter was waved to a chair while Beeler conferred in low tones with a heavy-set man in shirt sleeves who sat at a roll top desk.

"If you say he's all right, Beeler, why it's good enough for me," Tighe said formally. "I hope you enjoy your stay with us, Mr. Alcorn."

"Shouldn't take long to get what I want out of the prisoner," Lassiter said casually, and fervently hoped that this would be true.

Tighe said, "I assume you searched him for weapons, Beeler?"

"I can tell he's got nothing at his belt or under his coat."

Tighe nodded approval. "I hope your business with Tarsh proves satisfactory, Mr. Alcorn."

"Our readers are interested in how a successful rustler operates," Lassiter said.

Tighe showed large teeth. "Tarsh wasn't too successful. He got caught."

Beeler gave a bellow of laughter and Lassiter chuckled. "You're right there, Mr. Tighe," Lassiter said.

Lassiter got to his feet, hat in hand. The pants of the black suit were a little tight. He hoped that the .44 lashed to his leg didn't show through the trousers. But he didn't dare look down to make sure.

Beeler and Tighe had another few words that Lassiter couldn't make out. Then Beeler was beckoning and he led Lassiter out another door and along a corridor, their hells echoing against the thick walls. Lassiter still smelled a trap, but at this stage of the dangerous game he had elected to play he didn't know what could be done about it. A trusty mopping a hallway stepped aside to let them pass. One eye was swollen shut and the sullen face bore numerous bruises.

"I hope your editor isn't one to dig up dirt on so-called prison brutality," Beeler said pleasantly.

"An interview with Tarsh is all I'm here for."

"Fine. These prisoners are the toughest in the Southwest. Have to handle 'em tough."

"Sure looks as if the one with the mop was handled," Lassiter said, retaining his smile.

"There's some who say they'd rather have the noose," Beeler said pleasantly as they walked, "than spend twenty years here."

"I wouldn't like to spend any time in here," was Lassiter's comment. Beeler chuckled; Lassiter didn't like the sound of it.

The corridor seemed endless. Lassiter saw no cells, only stone walls on either side. They met no one on their march.

Just when he was beginning to wonder where Beeler was taking him, the captain halted in front of a solid door. Beeler unlocked the door with a large brass key, opened it to a squeal of hinges, then gestured for Lassiter to enter. Lassiter's nerves tightened. All he could see in the light of a flickering bracket lamp was a flight of stone steps. When Lassiter hesitated, Beeler spoke sharply.

"Thought you wanted to interview Tarsh."

"Doesn't look like anybody's down there!" Lassiter stood on tiptoe and peered down into the shadows.

"Tarsh is likely having a nap. Go ahead, Mr. Alcorn. Nothing going to hurt you."

Sweating, Lassiter started carefully down the steep stairs, mindful of tricky shadows. When he was halfway down he knew what to call the room at the bottom of the stairs: the "hole." It was some ten-by-twenty, furnished with cot, bench and a bucket. There was a odor of urine and sweat and cold stone of the walls and door.

"No Tarsh here," Lassiter said, trying to sound calm. He turned and looked at the captain of the guards who stood at the foot of the stairs, holding a gun.

"What's the idea, Beeler?"

"The idea is that you took me for a fool." Beeler's manner had changed. He was no longer the affable captain showing a visiting newspaperman the courtesy of the prison. In the flickering light of the bracket lamp midway up the stairs, Lassiter could see the thick neck slick with sweat. Lassiter felt his own sweat under the second-hand suit, some of it cold with apprehension. He was also aware of the steady boom of his own heartbeat in the windowless cell with its dank air and sounds of rats and mice scurrying somewhere out of sight.

Beeler said, "Pull up your right pant leg. Unfasten that gun. Do something foolish and you'll never leave here alive."

Lassiter considered arguing, but the gun leveled at his midriff decided him to play along. He knew Beeler could kill him and no questions asked. They said that Sheriff Ernie Joplin was the only honest politician in this southern half of the territory, but Lassiter knew that would be of little consolation in his present predicament, even if it were true.

There was nothing to do but obey Beeler's order. Lassiter sat on the bench, pulled up his pant leg and untied the .44. Beeler ordered him to place it on the floor and kick it over to him.

"Kick it gently, Lassiter, very gently."

Lassiter did as he was told; there was no alternative. Then he said, "How come you called me . . . was it Lassiter?"

"Tarsh had given up on you. But I figured you still might show up. I remember seein' you around here when you went to work for old man Ormsby."

"But you're mistaken. I'm Ben Alcorn."

"Start talking, Lassiter!"

Lassiter managed a blank look. "Talk about what?"

"Redgate's gold."

"Look, I don't know what you're talking about. I work for a newspaper and—"

"There's a million dollars in gold somewhere out in the Furnace."

Lassiter tried to make his scornful laughter sound genuine. And it wasn't hard because he'd laughed at the Redgate gold so many times himself over the years. "You believe those crazy stories?" he asked incredulously.

"This story I believe. Fella named Gil Ryan does work for a newspaper. Was here a couple of times to see Tarsh. I talked to him. Ryan claims that Colonel Redgate looted the Empire Mine . . ."

"That's an old story."

"Shut up and listen, Lassiter!" Beeler went on to tell how descendants and some of the original stockholders of the bankrupted mine were trying to locate the missing bullion. "Ryan says two of those stockholders came down here a few years back, trying to find that bullion. They went into the Furnace. They were never heard from again. They didn't know where the gold was. But we do, don't we, Lassiter?" Beeler's grin revealed large yellowed teeth.

"The Furnace has swallowed up a lot of people."

"That's the only truth you've said so far, Lassiter."

Lassiter decided to try again. He said his name was Alcorn and he was here to interview a prisoner. "I think you'd better let me out of here before my editor—"

"Tarsh claims he knows where that money's hid. Does he, Lassiter?"

"I didn't realize Tarsh was connected with the missing gold. But it'll make a good newspaper story."

There was a metallic clicking in the silent room as Beeler, standing at the foot of the stone steps, cocked his gun. "Lassiter, you got one minute to make up your mind," Beeler said impatiently. "Either you talk, or I'll blow you right into that wall."

Lassiter could believe that, from the stories he'd heard about the place. He tried to stall for time, but Beeler's hand did not waver. The muzzle of the cocked .45 looked big as a cannon. Lassiter knew he had about ten seconds left of the minute. He knew he had to gamble.

"What if I do tell you what I know? What then?"

"I can get you and Tarsh out of here. Between the two of you, I figure you know where the money's hid."

Lassiter eyed the captain of guards, noting the eagerness in the yellow-brown eyes. He knew that if he and Tarsh did find the money, it would be the end of them. If Beeler had his way, that is. Beeler was the kind to hang a favorite maiden aunt over a slow fire if he thought it would net him a dollar profit.

A muted scream from deeper in the big stone building prompted Beeler to say, "Seems some poor bastard broke one of our rules. Better make up your mind, Lassiter."

"Yeah." Lassiter began to talk, choosing his words. He spoke of the eccentric known as Leland Ormsby. "He claimed he was Redgate, but I didn't believe him."

"Where's the money?"

"Beeler, I don't know."

"There's something to that story of the gold or you wouldn't risk your neck getting into this place. You might've got away with it if I hadn't been halfway expecting you."

"You're too smart," Lassiter said.

"Don't try to butter me up."

Despite his precarious position, Lassiter almost smiled. Trying to flatter a hard nose like Beeler would be a waste of time. Lassiter didn't try it again. He found himself breathing shallowly of the foul air in this underground cell.

Lassiter tried to explain his position in the Redgate business. How it had been a Redgate map that had brought him to Ormsby-Redgate in the first place. He related how the old man stripped his range of cattle and later tried to kill him with a trick gun. "Sure I thought there was money around there someplace. But when he tried to tell me he was Colonel Redgate, it was too much. But where the gold is, your guess is as good as mine."

He shrugged elaborately, wondering if he could dive under Beeler's gun, reach his own .44 still on the floor without having the back of his head blown open. He decided not to chance it. He had walked with his eyes open into a trap. There was no law that had compelled him to visit Tarsh in this infamous pile of rock. All he could do now was wait for a break.

Roy Heeler gave him a tight grin. "We'll get the money. One way or another." Keeping an eye on Lassiter, he stooped, picked up the .44 and shoved it into his belt. "Climb the stairs. You first."

Lassiter wondered if he should try to jump Beeler at the top of the stairs. But Beeler had the .45 trained on his back.

Beeler made him stand aside, unlocked the door, and peered carefully along both sides of the corridor. "Want to make sure there's nobody around," he said, more to himself than to Lassiter.

Lassiter was curious. "You run the place. Why should you care?"

Beeler turned and eyed him coldly. "It's you I don't want seen. Not now, anyhow."

"You mean I wasn't s'posed to come out of the 'hole' alive?" Lassiter's laughter was as chilling as Beeler's eye.

"Just walk straight ahead and keep your mouth shut," Beeler ordered.

Lassiter stepped out into a corridor. It was the same one they had taken to arrive at the "hole" only this time they went deeper into the prison. Here there were no cells, just rock walls and Lassiter realized the corridor was in reality a tunnel cut through solid rock.

The skin at the back of Lassiter's neck prickled coldly. He had almost tried to jump Beeler at the head of the stairs. But there was no telling who might have been beyond the door. He recalled the guard at the gate with the shotgun. But there was no sign of guards now, nor of trusties mopping floors.

"Where we going now?" Lassiter wanted to know.

"Back here is where we keep the special ones." Beeler laughed and nudged Lassiter's backbone with the .45.

Beeler paused to close a heavy door and lock it. Then they proceeded down the corridor for another twenty feet. Here were three cells. On two of them the heavy outer doors hung open. The third one was shut tight. Lassiter looked through the bars of the nearest cell and saw the yellow-haired Joe Tarsh. At sight of Lassiter his mouth fell open in surprise. His hair as well as the thick mustache needed trimming. His once fine green silk shirt was dirty and ripped down one side.

"I figured you wouldn't show up, Lassiter," he said when he had recovered from the shock of the tall, dark man's sudden appearance with the captain of the guards.

Beeler unlocked the cell door and marched Lassiter inside. But not before a prisoner in the other cell spoke through the bars. "Lassiter, remember me?"

Lassiter looked around. At first he didn't recognize Deacon Hipp. The gambler and gunslick had lost weight, as had Tarsh. Hipp was grinning. A neat row of large teeth always reminded Lassiter of tombstones. The last time he had seen Hipp was at least five years ago, at the Double Ace in El Paso when two hardcases had tried to draw against him. The Deacon had killed them both, then fled across the river to Juarez. Lassiter gave him a cold nod, also remembering that Hipp had been suspected of killing a girl up near Santa Fe.

Beeler stepped out and slammed the heavy solid door against the bar of Hipp's cell door. "That takes care of Deacon Hipp," Beeler said, starting back to Tarsh's cell.

"The hell it does," came Hipp's muffled voice through the door. "You hombres got plans. They better include me!"

"Keep it shut, Deacon," Beeler warned, shaking a fist at the solid door. "Or the graveyard detail will be back here to dump you into a box.'

Hipp's laughter exploded around the hinged side of the door where there was a half-inch gap—sloppy workmanship from the political cronies who had slung this monstrous structure together.

Beeler returned to Tarsh's cell where Lassiter stood with his back to the wall. Tarsh's eyes were a little wild as if Lassiter's belated appearance, although anticipated at one time, had upset carefully laid plans. Beeler closed the door to Tarsh's cell. Lassiter felt a chill when he heard the clang of metal. Jail doors had always produced such a reaction in him. But this time a prison official shared the cell.

Beeler was saying tensely, "There's bookkeepers working here this week and I don't want trouble. You understand, Lassiter?"

"From the territorial capital?" Lassiter asked innocently.

"When I get my hands on Redgate's gold it won't make a damn bit of difference what they find."

As if to call attention to his presence, Deacon Hipp started hammering on the heavy door of his cell and shouting obscenities.

"I know what you got planned!" Lassiter heard him shout and took heart when he saw Beeler turn red and the lips under the mustache thinned as a razor slit. Beeler seemed on the verge of losing his temper.

"Sounds like I might have to shut him up," Beeler snarled.

He started for the door to Tarsh's cell, obviously intending to cross over and either threaten Hipp to silence or shoot him. Lassiter moved so swiftly that Beeler had no chance to react. One hand pinned Beeler's wrist holding the .45. The other hand snaked around, seized the .44 from the waistband of Beeler's trousers. Lassiter rammed the muzzle against a cheekbone.

"You better remember where you are, Lassiter!" Beeler cried, cranking his head around to glare back at Lassiter. "In my prison, by God!"

"You better get a cinch on that tongue or you won't have much of a face left," Lassiter warned.

Beeler rolled his eyes to the gun now ramming even harder against the cheekbone. "You're a crazy fool if you figure you can get away."

Lassiter grabbed the .45 in his left hand, then spun Beeler back against the wall.

Tarsh was agitated. "This ain't the way it's s'posed to be done, Lassiter."

"It's the way I'm doing it." Lassiter glared at Tarsh. A few weeks in the Fortress had already begun to whittle at flesh and nerves. "You should have waited. And not tried to deal Beeler into our game."

"Another week in here an' he'd have had me six feet under."

Lassiter couldn't argue against that although he secretly suspected Tarsh had lost his nerve. "How do we get out of here?"

"Beeler's got everything planned. You better give him back his gun."

"So he can use my backbone for a bull's eye. And yours too. Once he gets his hands on that money."

"Now wait a minute," Beeler said, trying to keep a faint whine of fear out of his voice. "We're all in this together."

"That's right, Lassiter," Tarsh put in, sounding eager. "Like I already told you once, I admit tryin' to steal the cattle money. An' I did get riled up on account of Claire. But now we're both on the same side of the creek." He put out his hand, but Lassiter wasn't about to give him a chance to try grabbing one of the guns.

Lassiter had already stepped into a trap and it was anybody's guess as to just how he was going to get out of it. He knew that no matter what, Beeler planned for him to end up dead. His mouth was dry; he was on edge. He didn't know the prison routine. Were guards supposed to look in on the prisoners at certain times? Even Beeler seemed apprehensive.

Lassiter said, "How were you figuring to get out of this place? I want to hear details, damn it!"

Tarsh mentioned the unoccupied cell. Nearly a year ago two prisoners had tunneled under the prison wall and to a ravine. Before they could make good their escape the Gatling gun from the nearest tower cut them to pieces.

"Beeler never filled in the tunnel," Tarsh explained tensely. "Anybody in here with enough dinero can buy his way out."

Beeler took over. "Better than leaving by the front gate. Nobody knows anything but me and my brother-in-law Tighe. The prisoners are marked 'deceased' and that's the end of it."

"I figured it had to be something like that," Lassiter said.

Beeler's smile was forced; sweat glistened through his mustache. "Now give me back my gun and we'll be on our way."

Lassiter shook his head. "No."

Beeler said, "We've got to have horses. My job was to leave them at the tunnel mouth. I go out front without my gun and somebody's goin' to wonder why."

"We'll pick up horses," Lassiter said flatly. "Someplace."

A drop of sweat rolled off the tip of Beeler's nose. "You can't go off half-cocked like this, Lassiter." Beeler's voice was low, intense. "It takes planning."

"When you had a gun on me, you said we'd go ahead, remember?" Lassiter said thinly. "Now that I've got it on you, you want to change everything." Lassiter showed his teeth. "Lead the way, amigo."

Tarsh lifted a warning hand. "Beeler's s'posed to give the guards in the tower some signal, so he claims. If he don't, they're liable to start cranking bullets outa that big gun."

"We'll find cover. Tarsh says there's a ravine."

"Hombres that built the tunnel," Tarsh put in, "made a mistake. They stood up to look around. Dead!" Tarsh laughed.

Beeler said, "Supposin' we do get out? We can't make it to the Furnace without horses."

And right then Hipp started yelling again, rattling the loose door on its hinges. Lassiter knew he had to make a decision. If Hipp kept up that racket, it would draw attention to this isolated wing of the prison.

"Keep it quiet, Hipp," Lassiter called to him. "We don't need any nosey guards back here."

Hipp recognized Lassiter's voice. "I'm goin' with you! Either that or I keep on yellin'."

"You're coming along, Hipp," Lassiter agreed and the outlaw gave a hoot of triumph. Lassiter wasn't pleased, but there was nothing else to do under the circumstances. He was remembering stories he had heard about the outlaw concerning a certain dead girl.

"I knew you'd figure somethin' out, Lassiter," Hipp called.

Beeler gave Lassiter a look. "You're crazier than I thought. To get Hipp mixed up in our business."

"I'd trust him a little farther than I would you. But that's not saying a hell of a lot."

Cords stood out in Beeler's bull neck. "If I holler, you're dead."

"Don't forget the bookkeepers you said are prowling around here," Lassiter reminded with a tight smile. "If there are any at all, that is." Then he added soberly, "All we've got to do is play our cards close to the vest."

"You're gonna make a mess of everything, Lassiter," Beeler said.

"Unlock Hipp's door, then we'll find us that tunnel."

Beeler looked angered and exasperated and a little fearful. "At least gimme back my gun. Hipp hates my guts."

"I'm not very fond of you myself." Lassiter gave Beeler a shove and at the same time kept one eye on the big blond Tarsh. There was no telling just how

Tarsh might decide to play his cards. The three of them crowded out into the corridor. The door at the other end was still closed. They were safe for the moment unless someone unlocked it and peered in to check on one thing or another.

When Hipp was released, the outlaw came out of his cell, grinning at Beeler. He held out a bony hand to Lassiter. "I'll take one of them guns."

"I keep the arsenal," Lassiter said.

Hipp started to argue. "I'm on your side."

Lassiter ignored him. He ordered Beeler to unlock the door of the unoccupied cell. Beneath the cot were some planks that covered a hole in the floor. Tarsh pulled the cot aside. The maw of a tunnel was revealed, chiseled out of solid stone and now faintly rimmed with dirt. It dropped straight down for three feet or so then angled eastward.

Lassiter issued instructions. "Tarsh, you go first. Beeler next. Then Hipp."

Tarsh turned on him, his mouth twisted under the ragged blond mustache. "Why the hell are you the one to give orders."

"Because I've got the authority. Two guns." Lassiter tapped the .45 in his belt with a forefinger, and waved the .44 under Tarsh's nose. "Main thing now is to get out of here."

Tarsh grunted, got down on hands and knees, and began to swear when Lassiter prodded him with his boots. He disappeared.

"They cut loose with that Gatling gun," Beeler argued, "there won't be enough left of us to put in a bottle. You better let me go fix things up with Tighe."

"Damn it, Beeler, get in that tunnel!"

Beeler dropped headfirst into the tunnel, then began to worm his way out of sight. Then it was Hipp's turn.

Lassiter had to remove his hat because the crown was too high for the tunnel roof. Putting both guns in his belt, he began crawling into darkness. He kept his distance from Hipp just so the outlaw didn't try to take it into his head to kick him in the face and try to get one of the guns.

"When we get there, Beeler," Lassiter called softly, "you keep your mouth shut. Remember, if there's any shooting, you'll get it first." He hoped the threat made an impression.

Beeler only grunted something and continued crawling. Wild animals had explored the tunnel, leaving their strong scent. He thought of the pair of convicts who had labored to chisel their way through the stone floor and dig the tunnel. Only to be cut down. The tunnel left intact so that Beeler and his brother-in-law Silas Tighe could bleed those prisoners with outside connections that could produce large sums of money in exchange for an escape.

Dirt trickled down the back of Lassiter's neck. He tried to throw off a trapped feeling induced by the narrow tunnel. His stomach felt hollow and his backbone was ice. What if rains had weakened the tunnel roof? That was a constant worry. To be buried under tons of earth with a convicted rustler, a bandit and murderer, and a corrupt captain of prison guards. Hell of a way to aid it all, Lassiter, was the thought that kept crowding through his mind. But he pushed it aside and concentrated on what lay ahead. Tarsh cursed the dirt that kept falling into his hair. It was dark as the inside of a sealed barrel. They crawled, grunted, and cursed rocks that bruised their hands and kneecaps. There was no turning back in the cramped tunnel.

At last Tarsh sang out, "Daylight ahead."

Lassiter could see it now by peering over all three heads. Beeler, in the lead, was parting some thick brush. "Tarsh, you hear me?" Lassiter called out.

"Yeah."

"Throw Beeler down and sit on him. Keep him quiet."

Now that he was only a few feet from freedom, Tarsh reverted to his usual cockiness. "I'll sit on his head, by gad. Ain't forgot how he beat the hell outa me with a rope end."

"Had a sample of that myself," Hipp cut in.

Lassiter scrambled as fast as he could to reach the tunnel mouth, dropped into a dry wash some three feet deep, and waited tensely. Tarsh was holding Beeler to the ground with the weight of his body. Hipp was lying flat.

Lassiter had drawn his gun just in case one of them tried to jump him. But Tarsh and Hipp seemed only interested in keeping down so that they did not attract the attention of tower guards.

If any of them stood up and tried to run, they would be spotted.

"We stay right here," Lassiter said, "till full dark."

"Hell, we can crawl an' make it," Hipp argued.

"Don't move, damn it. One of us gets careless and we're all dead." Lassiter glanced at the sky. It was only a matter of minutes till the last light was gone.

Beeler was strangely silent. Within the prison walls he was a strutting king, but out here he was just another man. Finally the waiting began to tell on his nerves. He tried to bluster, then threaten. Lassiter warned him that if he raised his voice and it carried to the guard tower, he was the first one dead.

After that, Beeler remained quiet.

When the last flaming redness on the horizon had been replaced by black velvet, Lassiter gave the order to move out. Again he warned Beeler not to try anything. They began crawling again, raising as little dust as possible. Even in the darkness it might be spotted by alert guards in the tower. After a quarter of a mile they could walk at a crouch. A few more yards and the dry wash deepened so that they could walk upright.

"Next thing is horses," Lassiter said. "Tarsh, you know this country. Any ideas?"

"The Bartlett place. Straight ahead." Tarsh began to chuckle. "Hey, Lassiter, by gad, you done it, you got us outa there. I tell you when I seen you come in the door with Beeler I figured the whole business was about to blow twice as high as the moon."

"We're not out of it yet," Lassiter cautioned.

Hipp was laughing. "We're out of it. But Beeler ain't."

"Leave him alone, Hipp," Lassiter warned. "I owe the sonofabitch for a few beatings."

"You heard me!"

Hipp showed his tombstone teeth in the light of an early moon. "You figure to give him a piece of the money, for Christ's sake?"

Lassiter looked at the tall, lank, grinning shadow. Then his gaze flicked to Tarsh who stood beside a rock outcropping. "What money you talking about, Hipp?"

Deacon Hipp laughed. "Redgate gold."

Lassiter turned on Joe Tarsh. "You talked too damn much!"

Tarsh lifted a shoulder. "Wasn't nobody back there to talk to but him. An', well, I told him. What the hell difference does it make now?" Tarsh demanded belligerently.

During the halt, Beeler had slumped to a flat-topped rock, breathing hard. He climbed to his feet, the broad face pasty in the wash of yellow moon. "Tell you what. Let's split the money four ways. It's over for me at the prison, anyhow." He put out a pleading band to Lassiter. "What do you say?"

Hardly had the last word left his mouth when he lunged. He made a frantic grab for the weapon Lassiter had thrust into his waistband. But Lassiter was ready for him. He ducked aside and starting to swing a fist at Beeler's heavy jaw when Hipp threw a rock. It was a large one and made a thunking sound as it struck Beeler at the base of the skull. Beeler fell face down, making no attempt to break his fall.

Drawing his gun, Lassiter covered Hipp, then crouched down to see how badly Beeler might be hurt. The guard hadn't uttered a sound. He turned Beeler over on his back. Beeler's wide eyes stared skyward, unblinking. Lassiter felt for a pulse. It was a waste of time.

"You killed him," Lassiter snarled, getting up.

Hipp said, "Now we only got to split the money three ways."

"You're wrong." And the barrel of Lassiter's .44 caught him on the temple. Hipp's knees buckled. He fell and rolled down a slight incline to come to rest beside the body of the man he had killed.

Tarsh clapped his hands together. "Hey, we got rid of two of 'em," he said happily. "Now there's only you an' me, Lassiter."

"Yeah, just you and me." Lassiter looked at the inert pair on the ground, one unconscious, one very dead.

"Gimme Beeler's gun," Tarsh urged. "We're partners now, for sure."

"Let's get us some horses and go dig up that money."

"No gun?" Tarsh scowled.

"Not till I see that money."

Tarsh braced his heavy shoulders. "What you aim to do when you see the gold, shoot me?"

Lassiter shook his head. "I give you my word I won't."

"How the hell do I know I can trust you?"

"I came back with Ormsby's cattle money, didn't I?"

Tarsh snorted. "Yeah. Come back to see Claire. An' on account of what you figured old man Ormsby buried around the place. Hell, she told me." Pinpoints of light glowed from the distant prison.

"When you were on the far side of the lake, in the trees?" Lassiter gave a cynical laugh, then said, "You carry Beeler's body."

Tarsh started to get mad, then eyed the .45 thrust in Lassiter's belt. "Beeler ain't no lightweight. You kin give me a hand."

"Get in close, you mean, so you can grab a gun. I keep the guns. You do the work. At least for now."

Tarsh grumbled and argued but finally gathered up Beeler's body. "Where to, master?"

"Where we can cave some dirt in on him."

"Better not be too far. He's a heavy sonofabitch." Tarsh struggled through the deep sand, weighted by the body of the corpulent captain of the guards.

The moon slid under a cloud and a breeze came up. Lassiter found what he was looking for, a spot where a cloudburst had undercut the bank of the dry wash they were traversing. Lassiter gave Tarsh instructions which were accepted with further grumbling. But he did as ordered and placed the body at the base of the sloping bank. Then Tarsh climbed up the bank, stomped his feet until sand and rocks caved in. It cascaded down on Beeler's body, covering it.

"I aimed to do Beeler in myself," Tarsh said, when he had scrambled back down the bank, his long blond hair flying. "Hipp done the job for me."

"I didn't give a damn for Beeler. But he should've had a chance to fight for his life. Every man deserves that."

Tarsh gave him a sidelong glance as they hurried in the direction of the Bartlett ranch where with any luck they might find horses.

"Wonder you lived so long in this country, thinkin' soft like that," Tarsh said with a shake of his head. "Hell, I believe in cuttin' trouble down afore it happens. Like Hipp done."

"Don't go pinning any medals on Hipp."

"The Deacon ain't so bad," Tarsh chuckled. "He'll be a mite surprised when he wakes up with a bad head. An' finds Beeler ain't layin' alongside."

"You a good horse thief, Tarsh?"

"One of the best."

"Then pick us a couple of good ones. I'll keep an eye on the house."

"While I do the work, huh? That again."

"I've got two guns," Lassiter reminded. "That makes me the boss. Cheer up and think of what we'll do with all the gold."

"You sure I can trust you?"

"Sure as shootin' you can."

"Shootin'? Hell, I don't like the sound of that."

Lassiter had to laugh; part of it was a letdown after the tension-ridden hours since he'd stepped inside the walls of the Fortress. There had been some minutes there behind those walls when Lassiter wondered if he'd ever get outside again. He stopped laughing, and looked at Tarsh stumbling along ahead of him down the gully. If Tarsh had kept his mouth shut, not spilled everything to Beeler.... Then he had to admit that Beeler had already sniffed the scent of gold and wasn't about to let Tarsh play the game alone.

Tarsh tried again on the subject of weapons. "Oughta have a gun, in case I run into trouble while I'm gettin' them hosses."

"I'll handle trouble, if any. You handle the horse stealing."

"You're a stubborn bastard, ain't you, Lassiter?"

"Been known to be."

The Bartlett ranch house was small, tucked into some rock slabs on a knoll that made it ideal for defense against enemies. Tank proved to be a good thief. He found a saddle rope hung over a post. Some horses loose in a fenced pasture were fairly easy to catch. Lassiter's mouth was dry as he kept one eye on the house, which was dark, and the other on their back-trail. How long would it be before the prison whistle started to blast the news that an escape had taken place? Or would it be kept quiet until Beeler could be located? Lassiter was under no illusions. If Beeler's body was found, uncovered by predators, he and Tarsh, as well as Hipp, could be charged as accessories in his murder.

Tarsh came up, leading one horse, riding another. In this country a man could be hanged for horse stealing quicker than for murder.

They kept the horses at a walk for over a mile so as not to alert the house because sound carried on the desert.

"When we've got our hands on the money," Lassiter said, "I'll see that Bartlett gets a better pair of horses than we stole."

"Lassiter, you're too damn honest."

"Not always."

Chapter Twelve

Bruce couldn't believe the change that had come over him; for the first time in his life he felt like a man. His father had more or less held him in contempt, Bruce always felt, because of his short stature. The Redgates were tall, robust men. And after marriage to Diana his self-image was even dimmer. She complained and carped and seemed to get no joy whatsoever out of their union. Nor had he, save for the release which came following the three nights a week she allowed him the privilege of being a husband.

Looking back, he knew he should have not lived so sheltered a life. His father had forbidden him to patronize prostitutes, stressing the degradation and possible disease. And yet he knew that that same father regularly visited certain women for hire. He had followed him on occasion, considered bringing the matter up, but always at the last minute his nerve failed.

But everything now was changed. He could look himself in the mirror of a morning and feel a certain pride in what he had accomplished. It was definitely a contrast to the day he and Diana arrived at OS ranch. He was surprised to see an attractive dark-haired young woman at the door. She invited them in. He introduced himself as Bruce Ormsby and asked for his grandfather.

"Your grandfather has disappeared," the young lady said gravely. "Some people think he might have been murdered."

This was just one more shock in a series of them since starting out for the West.

Diana said, "Now we can go back to some place exciting. Like Virginia City."

But Bruce wasn't even listening. The young woman, whom he learned was Claire Manning, seemed interested in him. He saw a warm smile and noticed how well she seemed to fit into the clinging black dress. As he listened to Claire tell of her role at the ranch as mistress, Bruce found himself blushing.

Diana was appalled. "An old man like that with a—a *mistress*?"

"I was quite fond of your grandfather, as he was of me."

"He wasn't my grandfather," Diana said, brushing back a lack of pale hair that had come loose from its pins. "He was Bruce's. And I don't see how you can sit there and calmly discuss your relationship with a man old enough—"

Claire finished it for her, "Old enough to be my grandfather." Claire laughed, revealing splendid teeth. Bruce liked the way the tip of her tongue would appear like a small pink animal, then dart from sight.

Claire was looking at Diana, who was red in the face and perspiring in her wrinkled dress. "Out here in the West, Mrs. Ormsby, you may change some of your ideas. What I did with Mr. Ormsby was far from sinful."

Bruce made his first decision since coming to the ranch. "The name isn't Ormsby. It's Redgate. And so was my grandfather's name. He changed it for one reason or another and insisted I do the same. Which I did. But now there's no use in keeping up the pretense."

Claire sat staring at him, wearing a faint smile. "Yes, *Redgate.* How nice to have you here."

Before Bruce could respond, Claire jumped up from the big Spanish chair, saying she would fix them something to eat. Then she was gone, leaving behind a tantalizing scent of perfume.

As he strolled about the big house that now belonged to him, he thought of the first time he had seen it at age ten when his father had brought him for a visit. In the first hour of their arrival his father and grandfather had shouted at each other in anger. It was because of the great conflict that Bruce and his father knew as the Civil War, but which the grandfather stubbornly referred to as the War Between the States. Grandfather had been a colonel under Beauregard, but Bruce's father had been unable to abide slavery and had gone north and later became a Union captain. Bruce's mother, who had died at his birth, had come south before the war and met Lansing Redgate.

"Ah am ashamed of mah own son!" Grandfather had raged at Bruce's father. "You suh, deserted your own kind and became a Yankee. And in so doing you disgraced our name."

"And so you changed it!" Bruce's father then added, "Perhaps for more reasons than so-called disgrace."

"Meanin' what, suh?"

Bruce's father refused to answer. Grandfather took young Bruce out on his private lake in a rowboat. "Ah made this lake so it would remind me of the bayous where ah was born. Do you know what a bayou is, Bruce?"

"I don't think so, sir."

Grandfather went on to explain in so syrupy an accent that Bruce had trouble following him.

"You spoke plainer when we first got here, Grandfather," Bruce said with the bluntness of a ten-year-old.

His grandfather pondered it a moment. "I'm trying to lose my accent. It's only when I get upset as I did with your father that I revert."

"Why would you want to lose your accent, Grandfather?"

"Put here I'm a new man, Leland Ormsby. I'm learning to speak like a damn Yankee. Or nearly so."

From the center of the lake Bruce could see the splendid house in the trees and behind it the barns and the bunkhouse. And where the lake made a V there was a dirt and rock dam and a silver splashing of water over the spillway that meandered along an old creek bed. A mile or so south it flowed underground, Brute was told. And out on the range, his grandfather continued, were four thousand head of cattle, everything handled by a crew of thirty men.

Grandfather spoke to the boy about the way things were when he had founded the ranch. "It was empty frontier. Sand, cactus, and rattlesnakes at the edge of the Furnace. And there was a sandy basin. I dammed the creek and made my own bayou. I built it all, Bruce. And it can be yours. I'd like you to live here with me."

Bruce was excited. But he knew his father would never give his permission. And he was too terrified of his father to even ask.

"Well, what do you say, my boy?"

"I . . . I would have to think it over, Grandfather."

"Bruce Ormsby. It has a fine sound. I would raise you as a gentleman."

"It does sound wonderful."

"And there is much more wealth here than meets the eye," the old man continued with a sly smile.

"Stay here with me and become Bruce Ormsby and one day when you're older I will reveal a secret that will make you rich as Midas."

Bruce finally did summon enough nerve to mention the conversation to his father. He was rewarded with a vicious backhand. "Your punishment for even considering such a vile proposal. I've always suspected the old fool was demented. Trying to steal my son is the final insult. We Redgates are going home."

But in his second visit to the ranch, eleven years later, Bruce found a vast change. The four thousand head of cattle were gone, the range stripped bare. There was no crew. And the house was in a state of disrepair, the plaster cracked, some of the floor tiles loose. Drapes were faded and torn. The leather furniture showed wear. Aside from a few head of horses, the only living thing on the ranch appeared to be a fiery dark-haired young lady named Claire.

After a meal of stringy beef and leftover beans, Bruce felt a little better. They were at the big table in the dining room. Diana had changed her clothes, washed her face and looked as presentable as Claire, he had to admit.

He found Claire watching him and felt he should clear one thing up. Diana had mentioned it while changing her clothes and he had to admit now that he thought it over, the whole thing did seem preposterous.

"You didn't mean what you implied about your relationship with my grandfather," Bruce managed to get out.

"I was his mistress." Claire gave Bruce and his young bride a defiant grin.

Bruce was embarrassed and also stimulated by her boldness. But he sensed his color was not as high as

Diana's. She looked as if she might topple from her chair in a dead faint.

Bruce embarrassed her even further by saying, "It does seem rather ridiculous to suggest that a man my grandfather's age would be interested in—er—in the female body."

"*Bruce!*" Diana cried. "What a horrible thing to say. To even *think* about."

Claire cocked an eyebrow and studied the blushing young lady in a strawberry pink satin dress, the waist nipped to extremes by a corset. Small diamonds caught sunlight at earlobes. She had a pretty but rather vapid face, light blue eyes and a pouting, roseate mouth. Claire had a feeling that in the bridal bed she had been untouched by fire. And her husband gave the appearance of having a backbone about as firm as a damp tortilla.

Bruce was storming about the big house, wringing his hands. His brown eyes puckered and threatened to fill with tears at any moment. Claire had just informed them bluntly of the rather sad state of affairs Bruce had inherited.

"But why would my grandfather strip his ranch of cattle?" Bruce cried. "And why did he let everything go to hell."

"A fact of life, I'm afraid, Mr. Redgate," Claire said smoothly, smiling. "But we'll make the best of it. Won't we?"

Claire liked the feel of that name rolling across her mind like a runaway barrel on a hillside. Redgate! And as close as she had been to that ancient bag of bones, gratifying his every wish, repugnant as some might have been, he had never told her his real name.

And she had thought there at the last that he might have known Colonel Redgate at one time. Quite possibly he had found that old pistol that was coated with black paint and which had Colonel Redgate etched on the heel plate. Of course, Ormsby and Redgate were one and the same.

Lassiter wouldn't be howling with laughter as he had the day she had mentioned Redgate gold.

That evening after dinner, Bruce spoke of his late grandfather telling him of wealth other than a ranch. "I wonder what he could have meant? I was ten, but I remember well him saying it."

Claire's heart nearly popped out of her breast. Wealth! If she ever needed a male partner it was now. Tarsh was imprisoned in the Fortress and Lassiter could be anyplace from Cheyenne to Vera Cruz.

Diana retired to one of the bedrooms, exhausted from the stagecoach trip. Claire suggested Bruce remain in the parlor so they could discuss his late grandfather and how to raise enough money to keep the ranch going. She hoped to feed him brandy and maybe loosen his tongue. And perhaps jog his memory concerning that "wealth other than the ranch."

He refused more than one brandy, saying that he had imbibed too much when they were in Virginia City and Diana had made him promise not to again.

But Claire did manage to get him into a bedroom at the opposite end of the house from the one occupied by his wife. Minimizing any chance she might overhear her husband's exuberant sounds of bliss. But all she could get out of him was a whimper. He was scared to death. And although she tried every maneuver that had never failed to arouse a companion, with Bruce Redgate she failed miserably. And he was equally miserable and humiliated by his failure as well.

Claire wondered if the nervous young bride was still a virgin. Claire almost laughed, then caught herself in time. She was not one to accept defeat easily. She would try again. She did successfully.

Things started to happen rapidly. Joe Tarsh wrote her from the prison. She visited him, promised to try and reach Lassiter. And Lassiter, bless him, had showed up here at the ranch as damnably attractive as always. The wheels were spinning now. She expected him back from the prison any day with news of the missing fortune that would make them rich.

But when Lassiter failed to arrive, Claire began to fret. Of course he had said there were certain preliminaries that had to be taken care of if he was to get inside the prison posing as Ben Alcorn, newspaperman. But surely it wouldn't take this long.

The same day that Claire began to worry more than usual, they had a visitor. He introduced himself as Gilbert R. Ryan. Claire was suspicious of him. He was tall and slender and rather good-looking, but there was something furtive about him.

While she stood talking to him in the doorway, Bruce happened to come into the entry hall. He shouted, "Gil Ryan! What are you doing down here?"

"Just happened to be in this part of the territory and thought I'd look you up!"

Claire didn't accept that, but Bruce did. Turning his head he shouted for Diana. "Honey, this is the newspaperman I met in Virginia City!"

Diana actually beamed. "Virginia City," saying it almost reverently. "Yes, of course I remember."

"I happened to see you and your husband arrive in Virginia City, Mrs. Ormsby. I remember telling your husband that I thought he had a beautiful wife."

"It's Mrs. Redgate," Diana said, beaming up into his face.

"I decided to go with the family name after all, Gil," Bruce explained.

"Why not?" But he was looking into Diana's blue eyes.

Gil Ryan stayed overnight. The following day, Diana Redgate and young Ryan were missing from the ranch.

They didn't come back that night.

Silas Tighe heard the news of the escape while nervously pacing his office. One of the guards brought him word. The man spoke carefully, knowing that such things as escapes were arranged.

"Beeler's gone and so is Tarsh and that fella named Alcorn."

Tighe nodded, his long face grim. He knew the truth; Beeler had whispered it to him while the so-called newspaperman sat stiffly in a chair across the room. The man was an impostor, his real name Lassiter.

"An' Deacon Hipp's also gone," the guard reported.

"Well, well." Tighe gestured at the door. "Thank you, Jones. I'll look into the matter."

Jones made an about-face and left the office of the prison superintendent. The moment the door was closed, Tighe's manner changed. He was exuberant. The Redgate fortune was within grasping distance. His brother-in-law Beeler had assured him of that. And the fact that Lassiter was mixed up in it only made it more of a certainty. Lassiter was known to be a high-stakes gambler who only went for the big money. There was no bigger money at hand than the missing gold bullion from the Empire Mine, Virginia City, Nevada.

He got his hat, collected what few important papers he thought might be incriminating, and left the prison. He rode south. He would wait for Beeler at their prearranged rendezvous at Belleville. Should there be any sudden problems relating to the engineered escape all he had to do was step across the line and thumb his nose at United States law.

He didn't understand Deacon Hipp's part in it, but Beeler must have known what he was doing to take the convict along. Beeler intended, in the excitement of finding the gold, to kill the rest of them. Hipp being in the game would mean one more man to murder. But Beeler was up to it.

Tighe was in a joyful mood. It was a clear day with only a slight breeze. Some miles south where clouds mottled the sky was Mexico. Sanctuary. He would be leaving behind only a harridan of a sister-in-law whom Beeler had married. She was the sister of Tighe's late wife who had been equally obnoxious.

In Mexico with plenty of money at their disposal, he and Beeler would build new lives. Gold could buy anything. Young and fetching senoritas would be his initial investment.

Chapter Thirteen

"There it is!" Tarsh screamed, waving a long arm toward a hillside littered with rocks and shale. "I knew I'd find it!"

Lassiter leaned over the saddlehorn of the stolen horse to stare. He felt his pulse begin to throb. All day they had ridden the northern edge of the Furnace seeking landmarks Tarsh would remember. Lassiter was about to conclude that Tarsh was about as crazy as old man Ormsby-Redgate had been or was up to some slyness on his own. Waiting for a chance to get hold of a weapon and finish off his companion of the prison break.

Tarsh was spurring ahead, his horse throwing up gouts of sand. He sprang from the saddle and began feverishly to paw aside the rocks.

Lassiter moved up cautiously. He scanned the bleak desert, saw no sign of movement, and dismounted. There was a narrow slot in the hillside that Tarsh was trying desperately to enlarge.

"Reckon coyotes got a whiff of the old man's carcass an' dug their way in." Tarsh looked back over his shoulder, grinning. "They won't get much of a meal off skin an' bones. Lucky for us coyotes don't give a damn about gold, ain't it, Lassiter?"

"Yeah, lucky."

Lassiter saw Tarsh eyeing the waistline where Beeler's gun made a bulge against the belt. "Come on, gimme a hand!" Tarsh shouted.

"You're doing all right."

"Hell, I ain't goin' to make a grab for that gun."

"That's why I'm staying back here."

Tarsh gave a crazy laugh and flung himself back to the task of puffing aside the rocks with renewed fury. When the opening was wide enough to allow them to crawl in, Tarsh went first. Lassiter drew his gun and made sure Tarsh wasn't ready to bash his head in the minute he reached what appeared to be a cave.

But Tarsh was frantically running in circles around a coffin of polished wood that rested on slabs of granite. There was a buckboard, the front end smashed by a wall of rock. Lying under the broken tongue was what remained of a human body; chewed clothing and a few bones.

The missing Canfield, Lassiter thought, although there was no way of identifying such remains. On the floor of the cave was a shattered whiskey bottle. There were niches in the wall for candles. Wax had dripped down the stone walls.

"Here's the old man!" Tarsh shouted.

Lassiter stepped forward but kept his distance. There was even less left of the old man than there had been of the one under the wagon tongue. Tarsh held up a belt.

"It's the old man's!" he cried. "I seen it often enough when I worked for him."

While Tarsh searched what remained of the old man's clothing, Lassiter looked in the coffin. He saw a saber painted black and also a gun, the mate of the one he had recovered from Belleville and later hid in the trees on the far side of the lake before meeting Claire. In the coffin was also a .30-30 rifle. It was loaded. He took it.

Tarsh saw him with the rifle. "What you aim to do with that?" he demanded warily.

"Not blow out your backbone if we find the money," Lassiter said with a tight grin. "As you'd likely do to me."

"Hell no. I keep tellin' you that. Where the hell is the money?"

After an hour of searching the floor, the walls and even the low ceiling, Tarsh standing up in the coffin to run his hands over the arched roof of the vault, they found nothing. Tarsh even used rocks to knock the coffin apart. Nothing.

"It's not here," Lassiter said finally.

"Then where the hell is it? It's gotta be here."

Lassiter let him go over the cave again, even pawing through the rubble at the entrance. Again there was no sign of gold. And there was no possible hiding place in the cave. The walls and floor and ceiling were solid rock, save for the narrow vent. And that was so narrow that Tarsh could barely insert his hand in it.

"The old man hid his treasure someplace else," Lassiter finally had to admit. He looked around, felt a chill when he thought of the old man's original plans. To have company in his journey of death; the original intended companions to the next life, Lassiter and Claire. And when he turned against Claire and Lassiter was out of it, he tried to involve Tarsh in the macabre ritual. But that still didn't explain what had happened to the missing bullion.

It was late afternoon when Lassiter had had enough. "Make up your mind to it, Tarsh. There's no place here to hide all that gold."

"I'll get sledge hammers an' drills and start diggin' into these walls!" Tarsh shouted, his hard blue eyes still wild with the prospect of riches.

"Waste of time," Lassiter said, keeping his own excitement in check. Tarsh had had his shot at trying to find the money. Now Lassiter intended to have his.

"I figure to stay here till I find it." Tarsh gave him a long look. "You sure ain't been much help!"

"I've seen enough," Lassiter said coolly. "There's nothing here."

He began to back out of the narrow opening. He wanted one eye on Tarsh. Tarsh demanded to know where he was going, for Christ's sake. "To get some air for one thing," Lassiter responded. "It smells of death in here."

"You got some ideas about the money?" Tarsh demanded. His fingers were raw from handling the rocks. Dust coated his face, the pale eyebrows and mustache. His eyes were bloodshot.

"If the wind doesn't come up to cover our sign, Bartlett could track us down. Ever stop to think of that?"

"He's an old man. His an' his woman run that ranch."

"He might have friends. If I'm ever gonna be hung to a tree, it won't be for helping you steal horses." He told Tarsh he would leave the Ormsby rifle, but unloaded. The shells would be twenty yards or so down the trail. All he had to do was look for them.

Tarsh was already back at work by the time Lassiter rode away, frantically banging on the cave walls with a rock the size of his head.

Diana could not believe the depths of her own depravity. It had happened so suddenly, Gil Ryan's appearance at the ranch, his sympathy when she finally blurted out her own troubles, her humiliation. "My own husband is . . . is . . . intimate with that terrible woman. While I'm in the same house with them. I see the way they smile at each other when they think I'm not looking."

Tears finally spilled out of her and she found herself in Gil Ryan's arms.

"I'll take a chance on your husband shooting me," Ryan said firmly, "but I think I should help you get away. Do you have a family back east?"

She shook her head. They were standing in the trees by the lake. Sunlight glittered on the placid surface.

"We'll go to Tres Vidas," he said. "I'll put you on a stage for Virginia City."

"But I have no money."

"I'll take care of that," Ryan told her. He brushed back a lock of pale hair that had fallen across her forehead. "My sister lives there. I'll give you a letter to her and you can stay there. Until I clear up my business here and we can figure out what to do."

He felt sorry for her, such a pretty thing and so afraid. What a monstrous thing her husband was doing to her. That Claire Manning should be horsewhipped, and in his mind's eye he saw her stripped to the waist, the lash being applied. It made him hug Diana so hard that he felt her firm young body against his.

They did not return to the house but rode his horse, the two of them, to Tres Vidas. There they learned the northbound stage wasn't due for two days. Ryan got her a room at the hotel and one for himself down the hall. Diana hid in her room, afraid to go out. Her mind was filled with Victorian tales of avenging husbands. She and Ryan could be murdered even though they had done nothing disgraceful. Gil Ryan had been tender and considerate, had embraced her and given her a brotherly kiss. But even so, Bruce could shoot them both because of something known as "the unwritten law."

She had expected to leave Tres Vidas immediately or she would never have come with Ryan in the first place. That her departure had to be postponed was terrifying.

Ryan brought her some food and a bottle of wine. He didn't stay and eat with her because he said, "I'm onto something important. See you in the morning."

The food was tasteless, the meat greasy, the potatoes overdone, the beans faintly sour. But the wine helped.

When someone rapped on the door later her heart froze. "Bruce?" she called out in her fear. "Gil," was the response.

And she was so relieved that she hurried to the door, noticing that her feet didn't quite go where she wanted them to and that she bumped into furniture. She unlocked the door and flung it open.

Ryan came in, his face excited. He locked the door and showed her a map. She saw that it was very old, the creases worn thin. It was signed: "Where I buried my gold, Colonel Redgate." And there was a date, 1865. On the map was a settlement called Andover and some distance to the north in a place called the Furnace was a large X.

"I've never discussed my reason for being in this part of the territory with you, but this is it!" He slapped the map with the tips of his fingers, tearing it along one of the creases.

"But I don't understand, Gil. You mean Bruce's grandfather buried gold?"

"And I know where it is!"

"This map will tell you?" She was bewildered.

"I was next door in the cantina when I met this old Mexican. He spoke very little English but he showed me this map he had found and wanted my opinion as to its worth. Well, one thing led to another and I finally gave him a double eagle for it. In the morning I'm going to start looking for that gold."

"Don't leave me here alone!" she cried.

"The stage will be along day after tomorrow."

"Take me with you!"

"But the Furnace is nothing but desert, no place for a genteel young woman."

"I don't care, I—" The room suddenly spun. She weaved over and flopped down on the bed.

Gil Ryan noticed that the wine bottle was empty.

Diana could not believe it of herself but she had actually shared a hotel bed with a man she had known only slightly. But in the morning she felt strangely without guilt. No bliss to speak of, but no guilt.

While Gil Ryan was loading the last of the supplies in the wagon he had hired, she heard some men talking about a prison break. It seemed that two convicts had escaped and taken as hostages the captain of the guards and a newspaperman who had been at the prison to interview one of the convicts. Also missing was the superintendent of the prison, Silas Tighe.

When Gil climbed into the wagon and whipped up the team, she mentioned the newspaperman. "His name is Ben Alcorn. Maybe you know him."

Ryan shook his head. "Never heard of him."

His mind was filled with other things. The Redgate gold, and the demure young lady sharing the wagon seat. Last night she had not been so demure, he recalled.

"They think the prisoners and their hostages have fled to Mexico," Diana said as she clung to the seat brace because of the rough road.

"If they get across the border, they'll never be found."

Finally after a few miles of silence and dust, she said, "What we're doing is terrible, Gil."

"No it isn't. Your husband is a scoundrel." He spoke confidently of a lawyer in Virginia City and mentioned a word she had never allowed herself to even consider. Divorce!

Gil was so excited that he let the team get away from him. They veered from the road, with Diana screaming. As the tail of the wagon skidded sickeningly, she suddenly found herself flung headlong into a sand bank. The last she saw of the team was a great cloud of dust as they pounded off across the flats, dragging behind them the wagon tongue that had snapped off.

She sat up and brushed sand out of her hair and wiped it from her lips. Then she saw Gil. He was crumpled beyond the smashed wagon. He didn't move. Seeing a bloodied end of white bone jutting from his right arm tore a scream from her lips.

Sand was beginning to blow when Deacon Hipp dismounted in front of Belleville. He tied the horse he had stolen to the rack. Its owner had objected. A bullet under the left eye from the gun Hipp had snatched from the man's holster had ended that.

Hipp's hair was blowing, sand beginning to shush against the door as he pushed it open. Dan Rambert looked up from behind his bar. There was a fresh scar on Rambert's forehead. The few strands of red hair were pasted to the scalp as usual.

"Deacon!" Rambert cried. "I thought you were in the Fortress."

Hipp went over to the bar, spitting sand, showing his tombstone teeth. "I was in the Fortress." He leaned close. "Need some fellas I can trust." He mentioned the Redgate gold.

Rambert smiled. "I didn't realize you were interested in mythology." He set out a bottle and glass.

Hipp turned his head, saw the bony redhead Ginger at a table, smiling at him. "Where's Mollie?" he demanded of Rambert. "Soon's I have a drink I need a woman with a little padding on her frame. Then we'll talk business. But now I want Mollie."

"Upstairs." Lambert began to laugh.

"What's so damned funny?" Hipp demanded.

"The head of your prison is keeping her company at the moment," the former professor of Greek history informed the tall, angular outlaw.

Hipp stared. "You mean Tighe?"

Rambert nodded.

Hipp's eyes acquired a strange gleam. "I killed his goddamn brother-in-law."

Something made him look around. Silas Tighe had heard voices, crept partway down the stairs in his sock feet. He gripped a gun and the hammer was eared back.

"You killed *Beeler*?" he yelled. The gun in his hand roared, but Hipp was slapping the floor with chest and stomach when the bullet drilled a hole into the front of the bar. He fanned, three bullets from his awkward position. Only one of them hit Tighe, but it was enough. Tighe doubled up, dropping his gun, and plunged the rest of the way down the stairs.

Mollie came down the stairs, buttoning her dress, her face going pale as she stared at the widening pool of blood on the floor.

"Better get a saddlerope on his ankles," Rambert advised calmly, "and drag him across the line. Better he be found in Mexico than here."

Chapter Fourteen

Just before the wind came up, Lassiter saw the wheeling *zopilotes*, black-winged against an azure sky. He had hidden the old man's Remington and saber, both coated with black paint, and was heading out when he saw the vultures slowly circling. Something dead or dying had attracted the scavengers. He didn't have time to spare to ride up through a pass bisecting sand hills to make sure. Then he noticed the fresh tracks of a team and wagon that had recently headed in that direction.

And as he reined in to study the sign more clearly, he heard a woman's voice. "Help me, please help me!"

He reached for his gun, in case it might be a trap. What he saw was a bedraggled young woman coming at a run. She had lost one of her shoes and her pink dress was ripped at the shoulder.

Her voice revealed strain when she halted, panting, and told him what had happened. "His arm is broken and I don't know how to set it."

Seen up close, she was a pretty thing, despite a smudge on a cheek and her hair that had come unpinned and was now being tossed by the damnable wind that was just starting to blow. Leaning over in the saddle, Lassiter pulled her up in front of him and started slowly along the wheel tracks left by the wagon. "'Who are you, anyhow?"

"Diana Redgate . . . Ormsby. I'm beginning to wonder just who I am." She sounded despondent. There had been something familiar about her when he first saw the forlorn figure coming across the sand.

"I got a glimpse of you at the Ormsby ranch. You were on the veranda with your husband." He didn't mention that they had obviously been arguing that day. "I'm Lassiter."

She stiffened, tried to pull away from him and almost lost her balance. He grabbed her before she could fall off the horse.

She said angrily, "That awful woman mentioned your name."

"You mean Claire Manning?"

"And you're no better. She spoke of you as being tough and ruthless."

"I am—with people I don't like."

She hesitated, then said, "Nothing I have done since leaving New York has turned out right." She began to cry.

"Stop feeling sorry for yourself."

Before she could respond, they reached the overturned wagon. Lassiter swung down, pulled Diana into his arms. Then he turned to a man on the ground. Ryan, she had said his name was. Ryan, pale and obviously in pain, had come to his good elbow. He gripped an S&W .38. From what Lassiter could see, there was a bad break in the right arm.

"Put down the gun and let me have a look at your arm," Lassiter said.

"You better do as he says, Gil," Diana said at Lassiter's side. "I feel so helpless. I don't know anything about broken bones. Do you?"

"Give it a try. He needs a doctor but that's a hundred-mile ride." He knelt down and contemptuously brushed the S&W aside. In the same movement he seized the weapon and thrust it into his belt.

Then he went to work on the arm. He pulled the bone back into the flesh, fitted it together as best he could by the feel of it. Then he got some strips of splintered wood from the wagon bed that had crashed against a rock outcropping when it went over. He lashed the makeshift splints into place with his bandanna and one he found in Ryan's pocket. Diana ripped off the bottom of a petticoat to make a sling for the arm. She seemed embarrassed that the lace-edged strip of cloth was out in the open for all to see.

Sweat beaded Ryan's forehead when the job was finished. "I hope it's been set properly," he said through clenched teeth. "If it grows back crookedly . . ."

"Better than being dead," Lassiter said bluntly, and heard Diana gasp. "Which you would be soon. In the Furnace with no water and no horse. What're you doing out here, anyhow?"

Diana started to speak, but Ryan gave a quick shake of his head. "Don't say anything."

"But he only asked a civil question."

"Diana, do as I say!" Ryan winced, for in his agitation he had shifted the broken arm.

Diana said, "You don't have to scream at me. I think Lassiter has a perfect right—"

Ryan's head jerked around. "Lassiter!" he cried. "You, the legendary Lassiter?"

"Don't know about the legendary part," Lassiter said with a shrug.

"I remember reading about your exploits in Denver. Such as the one with the daughter of old Joe Rugo, the Silver King. You shot a man over her, as I recollect."

"Had to defend myself," Lassiter said laconically.

"Now I remember. You stole her away from her fiance and he came after you. Pretty contemptible act on your part, I must say," Ryan finished.

"About the same as stealing another man's wife."

Lassiter gave him a level look. Ryan started to lever himself up on his good arm, then fell back. Sweat popped out on his face.

"It wasn't like that at all," Ryan protested. "Her husband treated her shamefully."

"Maybe she wanted her own way all the time and he wasn't about to give in."

"You are contemptible!" Diana cried, springing to her feet.

Lassiter stood up, dusting his hands. "Wait a minute, both of you! I don't give a damn if you want to make Redgate a cuckold. If he hasn't got guts enough to keep his own wife, then—oh, the hell with it."

As Diana's face drained of color, Ryan said, "There's no cause for you to talk to us that way. You don't know the circumstances."

"I know this, *Mister* Ryan. I had to make a sudden I change of plans because this young lady asked for my help. All right, I gave it. If I hadn't come along, the chances are you wouldn't have lasted twenty-four hours. Not twelve hours, if the wind turns into a real sandstorm."

Diana gasped, and bit her lip. Ryan said nothing.

"I only asked out of curiosity," Lassiter continued, "why you're out here in the Furnace. Then you had to start in on me. My guess is it has something to do with Redgate gold. Or my name isn't Lassiter."

"You better tell him, Gil," Diana said, clenching her hands.

Between grunts of pain, Ryan spoke. When he came to the part about the old Mexican who had "found" a Redgate map, Lassiter gave a snort of disgust. "Tenderfoot."

"I am far from a tenderfoot," Ryan said indignantly. He told of being from Virginia City. "And that is as tough a mining town as you'll find out here."

"Then you should've known better than to buy a map. They likely had a good laugh after you left the cantina last night."

Diana glared. "That was cruel to say."

"Oh, shut up," Lassiter said in disgust.

"Don't you tell me to shut up!" she cried, her voice shaking with anger. "I'm getting tired of being like a rug in the parlor that everyone can just walk on!"

Tears sparkled in her eyes as Lassiter knelt to tighten the bindings on the splints. When he turned his back on her, she in anger and frustration, kicked him in the side. It was more annoying than painful. Before she could withdraw her foot, he caught the ankle. It threw her off balance. She sat down hard, her skirts ballooning.

Lassiter smiled as she indignantly flattened her skirts to her legs. He got to his feet. "I'll go see if I can find your team." He did spot her missing shoe. He dumped sand out of it and handed it to her. She snatched it away.

He hoped he might have as much luck finding the horses perhaps hung up by the wagon tongue that had been shattered in the spill. But there was no sign of them. He turned back, the wind no longer in his face. If it didn't increase, maybe they could make it out of the Furnace.

Upon returning to Ryan and the girl, he stated bluntly what had to be done. "We need an extra horse. I know where to get one. Mrs. Redgate and I will ride double. Ryan, you'll have to walk."

"That's inhuman," Diana said heatedly, "to make him walk when he's in pain."

"I expect it is," Lassiter agreed. "But if I meet the hombre who owns that horse I'm talking about, I want to be in a saddle, not afoot. And if I do meet him, I'll yell and you drop off, Mrs. Redgate. Hear me?"

"I'll walk with Gil. *If* you don't mind."

Lassiter shrugged. "Just follow the tracks of my horse. It's a little over two miles. If your legs fold on you, just sit down and wait."

"My legs will not fold." Diana thrust out her chin.

"If they do, I'll come back. Providing I'm in one piece."

That frightened her. "What do you mean?"

"The hombre who owns the horse I want to borrow may not be all that eager to give it up."

He dropped Ryan's .38 in the saddlebags beside the weapon he had taken from the late Roy Beeler. He rode out.

There was no sign of the horse where Tarsh had left it anchored to a slab of stone near the narrow entrance to the cave. Nor did he see Tarsh.

But he did hear his voice after wasting valuable time hunting time for him. The voice came at his back. "Get I your hands up, you sonofabitch! I seen you comin' an' circled back to see what you was up to!"

Lassiter lifted his hands shoulder high, holding the reins loosely in the left. He started to turn the horse, using knee pressure.

"Just set," Tarsh warned, "or I'll blow you right off that hoss." Tarsh was mounted, aiming a rifle. "Thanks for leavin' the old man's rifle. Took me some scratchin' to find them cartridges."

"You better hear me out, Tarsh," Lassiter said, still turning the horse.

"Hear you out about what?"

Lassiter spoke of the newspaperman, Ryan. "The one who saw you at the Fortress. He's out here looking for the gold. Somebody sold him a map."

Tarsh was scornful. "Smart newspaperman, that fella."

"He's got a broken arm. He's with a young lady, the wife of the old man's grandson. Mrs. Bruce Redgate."

"The hell."

"I'd like to borrow your horse to get them to Tres Vidas. I'll bring it back."

"An' what do I do while you're gone? Set an' whistle?"

"Wait in the cave."

"Naw, I got a better idea, Lassiter. You an' Ryan wait in the cave. I got an itch to see Claire." Tarsh cocked his head, grinning. "On the way, mebbe I'll get rid of a little of that itch, providin' I like the looks of this Redgate wench."

Lassiter knew it made about as much sense to try and appeal to Tarsh in his present wild mood as it would to coax raw meat from a grizzly. But he made it sound good, just to stall for time and wait for a break.

"Ryan needs rest after getting his arm cracked. And Mrs. Redgate can't be expected to hike to Tres Vidas."

"Ryan, that smart-talkin' bastard. Purty uppity when I seen him at the Fortress. Wish it was his neck 'stead of his arm."

"Wait in the cave for me, Joe. You've got a lot of good in you. Give those two young people a break."

"Tell you what, you bein' so generous an' all. You an' Ryan ride double. I'll take the Redgate gal on my hoss. We each go our own way."

Lassiter shook his head. Over Tarsh's shoulder he saw Diana struggling along the faint tracks in the sand, skirts lifted. She was alone. At that moment she saw him, came to a halt, head lifted, poised as a young fawn ready for flight.

"She rides with me, not you Joe," Lassiter snapped.

"Which means you don't trust me," Tarsh said with a laugh.

"I don't want to see her hurt."

"Why you all of a sudden give a damn about her?"

"She's Redgate's wife and he'll be worried."

Tarsh let loose with another hoot of laughter. "Married woman out here in the Furnace with Ryan. Ask me, she likes Ryan. An' if she does, she can like me just as well. One way or another," he added significantly.

"Joe, you're no rapist. Don't talk like one."

"Who said anything about rape? I'll get her with my charm. She anything to look at?"

"Turn around and see for yourself. She's standing back there a ways."

Tarsh made a half turn in the saddle to look back, then suspected an old trick and tried to swing back. But Lassiter's gun boomed, echoes rolling across the flatlands. Tarsh gave a yelp of pain as the rifle went flying out of his hands.

Then he was wheeling the horse, pounding away, somehow able to keep a grip on the reins with his numbed hand. Lassiter lifted his gun, saw Tarsh's broad back in the faded shirt. He lowered the weapon. A wild shot could kill either Tarsh or the horse.

Diana came at a run, her skirts dragging. "You could have killed him and you didn't." She paused, panting, to stare in awe up into his face.

"Shooting a man in the back isn't my specialty. And I couldn't go after him and leave you here. Where's Ryan?"

"Back there." She gestured over her shoulder.

Somehow he got them all back to Tres Vidas, with him walking most of the way, letting Ryan and the girl ride double. Occasionally she insisted on walking with Lassiter, limping because her feet hurt. He grudgingly began to believe she might have a shred of spunk after all. Even Ryan managed some stumbling steps every mile or so.

It was so late when they reached Tres Vidas that the hotel was closed. By banging on the door Lassiter was able to rouse a plump and bearded hotelman who recognized him. The man, pulling suspenders up over a night-shirt, unlocked the door and let them in.

Lassiter paid for three rooms out of his meager reserves, then put up the horse in the livery barn. There was a chance someone might spot the Bartlett brand, but he had to risk it. The Bartlett ranch was far to the south and perhaps no one up here knew that horses had been stolen.

Carrying the saddlebags, he went to his room. Next door was the usual noisy cantina crowd. But he was used to it; he fell asleep.

It was long past midnight when he heard someone rap lightly on the door. "Who is it?"

"Diana," came the whispered reply.

He drew his pants over his underwear, rubbed his hand over the itchy bristle of chest hair and unlocked the door.

"I'm afraid to be alone," she said hoarsely. There had been a fight at the cantina and a gunshot. Then loud voices and coarse laughter.

He closed and locked the door. She seemed embarrassed when he just stood there in a bar of moonlight, giving her his hard stare.

"I—I'd like to talk," she faltered.

He went over to the bed and sat down. "Talk about what?" he asked coolly.

"You think I'm bold? Coming here like this?"

He lit a cheroot and blew smoke from a tight corner of his mouth. "The bold part was when you ran off from your husband."

"It wasn't like it seems at all." She stood by the door nervously trying to smooth wrinkles from her dress. "I thought I couldn't stand it another minute. Gil, Mr. Ryan that is, promised to take me to Virginia City."

"Don't you have any folks?"

"I have no one except my husband."

"And he brought you west and the life out here is too hard," Lassiter finished for her. "That right?"

"I could have stood most anything if he hadn't gotten mixed up with that—that green-eyed female."

"Nothing wrong with Claire."

"Not much," Diana flung at him.

"She's an opportunist. As I am. We all are out here if we're to survive. Why don't you sit down? Sorry there's no chair."

"I really should go back to my room."

"You said you wanted to talk." There were more loud voices from the cantina, more laughter.

Diana hesitated then came over and sat gingerly on an edge of the bed as far from him as possible. "Do you blame me for being disappointed in Bruce? When he flaunts that woman under my nose?"

"Doesn't show much sense, I admit, when it's done under your roof."

She twisted slender hands, bit her lower lip. "I really don't know anything about marriage and what it's supposed to mean," she said after a silence hung between them.

"I'll have a talk with Claire and try to get her to leave your husband alone."

"Do you have that much influence with her?"

Lassiter gave a sidelong glance at the wide young eyes and said, "You might say I've got some influence."

Diana sighed. Loud voices from the cantina were beginning to fade. Nearby a dog started barking, probably at a drunk or maybe at the moon. Someone came up the stairs. There were hushed voices. Diana gasped when she saw Lassiter pick up the .44, cock it and wait. But out in the hallway a man laughed and a girl giggled. A door opened and closed. Lassiter slid his gun back under the pillow.

"Is there really anything to that Redgate gold?" Diana asked softly. "Or is it just a legend, like King Arthur's Court?"

"Yeah, I think there's something to it. Not at first, but it's grown on me." He gave a short laugh, then he said, "Best thing for you is to go back east where you'll be safe."

"But as I told you, I have no one."

He put his cigarillo on the edge of the washstand and took her hands. They were cold. "You must have friends."

"Not real friends. You see, I was raised by an uncle and he and Bruce's father made an arrangement, I guess you'd call it. That Bruce and I would marry. I went from school right into marriage."

Lassiter dropped her hands that were beginning to warm in his. It wasn't a time for involvement with a brittle female who might shatter like fine crystal if not handled just right. But she did make a fetching picture sitting there, hands now folded demurely in her lap.

"I've never met anyone quite like you," she said, not looking at him. "The way you shot the rifle out of that man's hands. He should thank you for not shooting him."

"He won't."

"You're enemies, I suppose."

"Now we are, for sure." Her nearness, the provocative bundle of flesh under the stained dress was reaching him deeply.

Sounds of a horse moving along the street claimed Lassiter's attention for a minute until they faded. At that point it seemed her scent, for some reason or other, seemed more pronounced.

When she started to get up, he suddenly took her by the wrist and pulled her against him, so that he felt the softness, the warmth. Expertly he caught her in an embrace, captured her full lips. For a moment he encountered resistance. Then the lips softened and began to move under his.

After a moment he drew back. "Is that what you came for?"

"Nonsense. I came to . . . to talk."

In the moonlight through the window her eyes were unusually bright, her lips relaxed and moist. And he knew what she needed; education in the ways of life as her husband should be receiving from the ambitious and uninhibited Claire.

As he kissed her again his fingers fumbled at side buttons of her dress. One of them came off and made a dull plop against the plank floor. At least she didn't talk and make further pronouncements of coming to his room after midnight only to hear the sound of his voice. Perhaps powers of speech had been locked in her throat. Her body was stiff as iron when he pressed her back upon the bed then deftly drew the dress over her head. Pins from her disarranged hair fell to the bed And she had taken such pains to pin it up after the experience in the Furnace. Her camisole was decorated with small blue ribbons.

She stared as if frozen with fear, her eyes wide. Goose bumps rose along her forearms and thighs.

"One way to warm you up," he said, kissed her shoulder. He maneuvered her to the center of the bed, covered her with the blankets, then got in beside her.

Pressure of his lips gradually eased the stiffness in her body, finally it collapsed under his weight. But she came alive and made a small outcry, overwhelmed by the surprising power of his maleness.

"Lassiter," she moaned, her breath warm against his neck. "Do you think me terrible?" But her voice drifted away as she was caught up in the passionate moment that stretched into a full hour.

"I never dreamed it could be like this," she gasped when they lay together, exhausted.

She repeated it when the first rosy hint of dawn was inching up the eastern horizon, then hurried back to her room.

When he went to wake up Ryan, Lassiter found the room empty. He found him in the cantina next door. Emilio Ruiz was sweeping up a pile of broken glass on the floor when Lassiter entered.

"A wild night in here, amigo," Lassiter said.

"The usual," Ruiz grunted.

"How long's he been here?" meaning Ryan, who was slumped at a table, head on the unbroken arm. The other in the sling was hugged to his body.

Ruiz looked at the bareheaded young man in the dusty clothing. "Midnight he come. Then I go home and sleep. He still here this morning. He a friend of yours?"

Lassiter gave a sharp laugh. He went over to Ryan and said, "I saw one drunk die before my eyes, don't make it two in a row." Lassiter stood, saddlebags slung over an arm, watching him.

Ryan lifted his head. His eyes were bloodshot. Although he reeked of mescal, he did not seem drunk. "You had her, didn't you?" he accused.

Lassiter straddled a chair. "Listen to me. Here's the story you tell when you get back to the ranch."

"I'm not going back."

"The hell you're not. You're facing up to her husband. You're telling him about the map. Diana wanted to help you find the gold. Find it for her husband. Understand?"

"He'll never believe that."

"*Make* him believe it. Tell him about the accident that broke your arm. You stayed all night on the desert. And nothing happened between you and his wife."

Ryan's lips twisted. "Maybe I should tell him about you and his wife."

"Do that!" Lassiter bared his teeth. The threat was implied and Ryan lost color. Then Lassiter said, "Convince her husband. After that, I don't give a damn what you do."

"What'll you be doing?"

Hunting for the Redgate gold. But Lassiter didn't voice it. Ryan asked for the return of his gun.

"You'll be hiring another wagon. I'll leave the gun at the livery barn."

"I suppose I'll have to pay for the one I wrecked and for the team that ran away."

"Could be worse. At least somebody isn't having to pay for your funeral."

Ryan turned the macabre thought over in his mind and said, "I agree. I do owe you my life."

Lassiter found Diana in front of the hotel, shading her eyes against the sun. A bright smile touched her lips when she saw him. "Lassiter!" she cried, seeming relaxed and happy. But her mood changed when Lassiter told her what was to be done.

"I'd rather go back to the ranch with you, instead of with Gil," she complained looking anxiously up into his face.

He shook his head. "Got to be this way." Then he stiffened. Down the street Joe Tarsh with the tangled pale hair, the untrimmed mustache, was dismounting. Tarsh saw him at the same moment. Tarsh's mouth slowly opened in surprise. Lassiter stood with the saddlebags containing the two revolvers, Beeler's and Ryan's, slung over an arm. Pushing Diana aside, he waited, poised, ready to draw the .44 if Tarsh made a threatening move.

But Tarsh came walking along the street toward the hotel. Lassiter spoke to Diana, "I told Ryan what to do. Follow his lead. Now get back inside the hotel."

"That man," she said in surprise, seeing Tarsh come thumping along the walk.

Lassiter shoved her inside and Tarsh halted as the hotel door swung shut. "Purty thing, ain't she?"

"If you had any brains, Tarsh, you'd be in Mexico by now," Lassiter said coldly.

"I need a gun. You broke the trigger on the old man's rifle with that shot. You damn near busted my thumb." He held up a bruised thumb.

"Let's get out of town," Lassiter said.

Twenty minutes later they were heading out across the Furnace, keeping their eyes open. Tarsh spoke for the first time since Lassiter had finished saddling his horse in the livery barn.

"Sorry I got all riled up at you yesterday," Tarsh grumbled, "but I figured to find that gold an' when we didn't—"

"Forget that part of it." Lassiter reined in. "Tarsh."

Tarsh looked around, pulled in his horse. "Yeah?" he asked suspiciously.

"I meant what I said about Mexico. Head for the line. I don't want you on this side."

"I try to be friends an' you start givin' orders."

"Friends?" Lassiter gave a hard laugh.

"Why the hell should I head for the border?"

"For one thing because I said so. Stay away from the Ormsby ranch. Leave those people alone. And besides, if you hang around here and Sheriff Joplin spots you, it's back in the Fortress."

"How about yourself? You escaped, same as me."

"But I wasn't a prisoner," Lassiter pointed out coldly. "Not officially."

Tarsh rubbed his chin. "Looky, I been thinkin'. There's dynamite at the ranch, in a shed like I told you once. We could grab it an' head back for that cave an' blow it all to hell. Bet the gold is there *someplace*!"

"You need to buy an earhorn if you're hard of hearing. I told you to stay away from that ranch."

"But the gold, damn it!"

"It's not in the cave, I'll bet on that."

Tarsh's diamond chip eyes bored into Lassiter's face. "Then where the hell *is* it?"

Lassiter sat his saddle, dark features implacable.

"Just don't push it, Tarsh," he warned. "Get out." Lassiter gestured south, toward the border. "Be thankful you're not doing that stretch in the Fortress. Be thankful for that much and forget about the gold."

"Ain't right to expect me to cross that border with no gun."

Lassiter reached into the saddlebags, unloaded Beeler's .45 and tossed it to Tarsh. "This time I keep the shells," he said with a tight grin.

Tarsh started to bluster again, took another close look at Lassiter's eyes, then turned his horse. The last Lassiter saw of him he was at a lope, leaving a trail of dust that drifted into the sky like beige-colored smoke. Lassiter had his own idea about the cave. Not the cave itself, but the area surrounding it. He and Tarsh had not explored the possibility that the old man might have buried his treasure close enough to the cave so he could visit the gold in spirit if not in the flesh.

But two days later he had found nothing. On the third he ate the last of the desert deer he had brought down with the .44 instead of a rifle.

Chapter Fifteen

In the parlor of OS ranch house, Deacon Hipp smiled at Diana. "You're a purty gal. Got a fine figure. But I ain't above spoilin' it. You see, I can buy any female I want with a million dollars."

Dan Rambert looked at him. "Your share isn't quite a million dollars," the Belleville saloonman reminded him coldly.

Hipp, straddling a chair, his long legs stretched out, ignored his friend. His attention was on Diana: "The old man wrote your husband about the ranch. Sent him a quit claim deed, all signed an' legal. So why in hell wouldn't he at the same time write about the gold?"

"He didn't!" Bruce cried. "I've told you. Leave her alone. Pick on me, if you want, not her."

"She's a sight purtier than you, son. You'll melt a lot faster seein' her blood than you will seein' your own. Leastwise that's the way I got it figured."

Rambert said, "I don't like this business of threatening a young lady."

Hipp cranked his head around, the long face stony. "Down at Belleville you deal in females."

"For dancing. What else they want to do is their own affair."

Thunder suddenly filled the house. It was Brownie Lock swinging a heavy sledge hammer against a wall. As adobe bricks crumbled, Sam Varney peered through the dust, hoping to find a hidden place that might conceal the lost gold.

Bruce lay face down on a sofa, his body arched like a drawn bow because of ankles and wrists roped together. These ruffians had descended on them without warning. Their first act was to lock Claire in a storeroom. Bruce's eyes roved wildly between Dan Rambert and the cold-eyed Hipp.

"Please don't hurt us," Bruce Redgate begged.

Hipp said coldly, "If you don't want to see your wife bare nekkid in front of us all then tell us where grandpa hid the gold. I'll give you plenty of time to make up your mind. Exactly one minute, sixty long seconds."

Hipp bound Diana's wrists in front of her with a length of rope, then pushed her onto another of the large sofas in the room. It was covered with fine grain leather and the frame was of heavy dark wood. Furniture for the mansion had come from Spain in the early days by way of New Mexico.

Hipp said, "Minute's up. Rambert, why don't you go in an' give Brownie a hand. Long as you seem so squeamish."

"I say it's not right."

"You shoulda stayed with Greek history, Dan. You got no stomach for this."

Rambert reddened.

At that same moment Lassiter was alerted. He had heard the booming sounds coming from the house as he was riding through the trees on the far side of the lake. At first he thought it was distant thunder he heard. Then as he cleared the trees he saw the four horses in the yard by the adobe wall of the veranda. The horses moved nervously around trailed reins as the booming sounds continued from the house.

A glance at the brands told Lassiter nothing. Dismounting, he drew his gun and ran lightly up the stone steps of the veranda. The front door was ajar. In a sudden cessation of the booming sounds, Lassiter heard a voice.

"All right, Dan. I'll give in. I'll let young Redgate about it for five minutes or so. I agree it'd be a shame to use a knife, 'less we have to." Then Hipp said, "Brownie, try the other wall."

Lassiter tiptoed into the parlor. Through a doorway he could see into a corridor where Dan Rambert stood watching a big, muscled man holding a sledge hammer.

"You have no right to destroy my property!" Bruce was protesting loudly. He was tied hand and foot, Lassiter noted. "You men are trespassing," Bruce finished in an anguished voice.

Deacon Hipp's gravelly laughter filled the house. His angular figure was clad in funereal black; almost a match for the second-hand suit Lassiter had worn in his masquerade as a newspaperman. After the escape from the Fortress he had unrolled his range clothes from a tarp and exchanged them for the suit. He had left the suit behind. He didn't care if he ever saw the damn suit again. It would always remind him of Beeler and the Fortress.

Lassiter recognized the man now holding the sledge hammer as Sam Varney who had fled Dan Rambert's saloon rather than tangle with Lassiter. And next to him stood Brownie, with shaggy brown hair and beard. His left shoulder sloped at an awkward angle, no doubt from the collarbone Lassiter's bullet had smashed that day.

When Varney swung the sledge against another section of wall, Bruce screamed. "You'll bring the roof down on us!"

Hipp laughed and said, "Your time's runnin' out, kid."

Lassiter stepped deeper into the room. Down a hallway he could see a bedroom part way open. Holes had been punched in all four of the walls was the way it looked to Lassiter.

Lassiter cautiously moved deeper into the parlor with its narrow windows, more for defense than sunlight. He saw Diana for the first time, huddled on a sofa, her bound wrists in the lap of a pale blue dress with a lace collar.

As Lassiter took another step, hoping to get into position so he could cover all four men at once, Brownie Lock turned his head at the wrong time.

"Lassiter!"

The room erupted. Varney started to fling aside the sledge hammer and reach for a gun. But Lassiter's bullet screamed off the blunt end of the sledge that was whitened with plaster. Brownie Lock dug for a gun and found Deacon Hipp in the way. But Varney had a weapon in play, flame spitting from its muzzle. Padding erupted from a chairback where Lassiter had been standing but a moment before.

Diana was screaming in terror but Lassiter had to concentrate on Varney. The man's bellow of pain overrode Diana's screams as Lassiter's gun roared. The power of the .44 slug slammed him against the wall he had ruined. As Diana continued to scream, Lassiter spun around with his gun to see what was frightening her. He froze when a bar of sunlight from a narrow window glittered on naked steel. A knife point at Diana's throat produced a tiny drop of blood. Its handle was gripped by Dean Hipp's long slender fingers. His yellowish eyes were challenging.

"Lassiter! You want to see *more* of her blood?" Hipp hovered over a terrified Diana. Only the slightest pressure of his hand would drive the knife point into the soft white throat.

No further threat was needed. Either Lassiter dropped his gun or Bruce's young wife was dead. Hipp would show about as much emotion killing a woman as he would in crushing an ant.

"All right, Deacon," Lassiter said in a tight voice. "Don't cut her any more."

Rambert, sweating under the sparse red hairs pasted to his pate, came over and kicked the .44 aside. "That was easier than I believed possible," he said, his voice showing strain.

Diana was rigid, the bound hands pressed to her lips as if to suppress further screams. Brownie Lock looked down at Sam Varney who was crumpled against the broken wall. Next to him was the heavy sledge that had done the damage.

Then Lock looked over at Lassiter. "I owe you for Sam. I owe you for this." He rubbed at the old wound at his collarbone.

"Heat an iron," Hipp ordered. "Lassiter knows where the gold is."

"What if he doesn't?" Rambert cut in.

"If we burn holes in his hide, he'll remember every damn thing the old man told him about the money." Hipp smiled at Lassiter. "'Fore you showed up we only had a pair of deuces. Not we got us a full house."

Lassiter's wrists were tied behind his back to one of the two posts supporting a lean-to from a barn. Under the sloping roof was the ranch blacksmith shop with its litter of barrels and horseshoes. An OS branding iron glowed cherry-red.

Brownie Lock pumped the bellows, hunched over because of the shattered collarbone that had not healed properly.

Diana had been brought to the yard. One end o a heavy rope looped about her waist was tied to ar anvil. Claire was marched from the house, the greer eyes sullen until she saw Lassiter tied to the post.

Hipp glared at her. "Never did figure out wha you're doin' around here," he snapped.

"She was the mistress of my husband's late grand- father," Diana said, her voice shaking. "Now my hus- band's mistress."

Claire showed her fine teeth. "You icy little bitch."

Hipp picked up the branding iron from its bed o coals. "Hot enough," he declared.

Diana's voice broke. "Oh, my God!"

"Lassiter, you better start talking," Dan Ramber urged. "Maybe I owe you for breaking my head witl a chair. But I don't necessarily like to watch your flesl start smoking from that branding iron."

Hipp grinned. "I like the way you put that, Dan." Hipp advanced with the glowing iron; Lassiter could feel its heat. Hipp said, "Lassiter, you got one chance Speak up, damn it!"

Claire paled and tried to protest, but Hipp shu her up and bared his tombstone teeth to Lassiter "Well, Lassiter, that iron'll burn through to you backbone. If you're dead, that gold won't do you a damn bit of good."

Claire was looking wildly around, probably for a gun, Lassiter guessed. She'd only get herself shot. He gave her a warning shake of the bead. Then he allowed himself to sag against the wrists bound to the post. He fought for breath, for control, then said, "Hipp, you're right. Dead, I can't spend a dime of that gold."

Hipp grinned. "I figured you had brains. For the first time you're usin' 'em."

He waited while Lassiter seemed to be trying to force enough strength back into his legs so he could stand upright again. Lassiter leaned back against the post; it gave slightly from his weight. "Deacon, I deserve some of that money."

"After we count it, we'll see," Hipp said impatiently. "Well, *talk*, goddamn it!"

"It's under the safe," Lassiter gasped.

"*Under* the safe!"

"In the ranch office," Lassiter said. "The old man figured it would be a job for anybody to move the safe to get at the gold."

Hipp turned his lean body to glare at Claire. "If you was the old man's mistress, you oughta know a few things. Is Lassiter tellin' the truth?"

"I do know this," Claire said, only a trace of tension in her voice. "The old man talked to Lassiter about the gold."

"You come along where we can keep an eye on you," Hipp snapped.

"Of course." She gave him a warm smile. "I know where he hid the key to the office. You won't have to break down the door."

Lassiter wanted to signal encouragement to Claire, but instead continued to hold his mask of apprehension. He knew she wasn't fooled. He said, "One thing for sure, sit at the old man's desk and you'll have a good view of them doing all that heavy work. And you'll be in the old man's chair when they see that first gleam of gold."

She looked at him, the tip of her tongue running across the lower lip. "The old man's chair, yes." Hipp shoved the branding iron under Lassiter's nose. "The money better be there." Then he flung the iron back into the bed of coals and picked up a crowbar. It had been leaning against the barn wall and was wreathed in cobwebs. "We'll move that goddamn safe. Brownie, you stay here an' keep an eye on Lassiter. Dan, you come along with me."

Then Hipp started marching Claire in the direction of the office. Her long black hair gleamed in the sunlight. Lassiter heard Brownie Lock mutter to Rambert, "Seems like the Deacon thinks he's takin' over."

"The gold is more important right now, Brownie." Lassiter saw Rambert wink broadly at the brown-bearded Lock. "Just set tight for now," he finished and hurried after Hipp who was walking rapidly on his long legs with Claire through some cottonwoods that screened the ranch office.

Lassiter watched Brownie Lock stare after them, a scowl on the bearded face as if he resented being left out of it.

"Should be a sight a man sees once in a lifetime," Lassiter said for Lock's benefit.

Lock looked around. "Sight of what?" he demanded.

"All that gold."

"Yeah?"

"You know what they say about possession being nine-tenths of the law. Was it me, I'd be there with Hipp and Rambert for that first look."

Lassiter's mouth dried as Lock checked the lashings that bound Lassiter's wrists to the supporting post of the lean-to. "If you're up to any tricks, Lassiter—" He broke off and drew his gun. "I oughta finish you off for what you done to Sam."

"And they'll likely finish you off. Once they get their hands on that gold."

Indecision twisted the bearded lips as he stood with the gun leveled at Lassiter's breastbone. It was Diana's plea that drew his attention away from Lassiter.

"Please don't shoot him. I—I could never like a man who committed cold-blooded murder." She tried to smile at him. "I . . . I'd do most anything if you didn't kill him."

And while Lock was studying her, his back turned, Lassiter pressed his weight back against the post. It gave even more than before.

"Ain't no sense tryin' to fool me," Lock said to Diana. "But reckon I will take a little of it right now." He holstered his gun, strode to where Diana was tied to the anvil. She put her bound hands over her mouth, but he brushed them aside.

At that moment came a great screeching from the direction of the ranch office; it was the safe being levered across the office floor by the crowbar in two pair of strong hands.

Lock wheeled and bounded away, shouting, "Redgate's gold! I sure wanta have the first look!"

Lassiter flung a hard look at Diana. "You tried," he said in a low voice. He stood, head cock, listening. There was more screeching. If Claire had only been able to get Hipp or Rambert in front of that desk and trip the trigger of the hidden gun. Perhaps both of them, if there was any luck this day at all. But now she had a third man to contend with, Lock.

Lassiter chose the moment of another screeching from the office to fling his weight against the lean-to post. A sound of rusted nails ripped from the roofing timbers was lost under the continued sounds from the office.

Diana stared in fascination, bound hands pressed against her hips, as Lassiter again thrust his weight against the post. And this time the rotted base snapped off at ground level so that without the supporting post the lean-to roof teetered precariously.

"Hurry!" Diana implored in a hoarse whisper.

Already Lassiter had slipped his bound wrists off the rotted end of the post, had whirled and was rushing into the house. In the kitchen he found a butcher knife and quickly went to work. Kneeling on the floor, the knife handle wedged between his feet, he began to saw lashings against the sharp blade. Steel cut into his flesh. He winced at the pain, but sawed away even harder. It seemed it took minutes instead of seconds to free himself. Hipp had taken his gun, so he had to look elsewhere. He found one of the ranch rifles on wall pegs near one of the narrow windows.

Bruce, still trussed up on the sofa, turned his head, eyes rolling as Lassiter approached with rifle and butcher knife. Lassiter quickly severed his bonds.

"Your wife's outside." He tossed the butcher knife onto the sofa. "Cut her loose!"

Bruce rubbed his wrists to restore circulation, saying, "I should have a weapon of some kind."

"Find one!"

Lassiter didn't even look around. After making sure the rifle was loaded, he slipped from the house. Brownie Lock was just coming around a corner of the building from the direction of the ranch office when he spotted trouble. One glimpse was all he needed; a corner of the lean-to roof where the supporting post had been snapped off. And no Lassiter.

At sight of his drawn gun, Diana began to scream in terror again. Lock ignored her, but it did warn Lassiter in the house. Lock turned his head and shouted two words toward the office: *"Lassiter's gone!"*

It was all that was needed. Rambert rushed from the office, shouting angrily, "Brownie, why'd you let him get away!"

But the roar of Brownie Lock's gun drowned out anything Rambert might have added. Lock had spotted Lassiter coming at a run, and snapped off two quick shots.

Lassiter heard the crack of the bullets against the house wall. Bits of plaster slapped the side of his neck. Rambert was in sight by then, pounding up from the office, the face with its fresh forehead scar sweated from the exertion of levering the heavy safe across the floor with a crowbar. Rambert's mouth was already open in his angry shout at Lock.

Lassiter dropped to one knee just before the third bullet from Brownie Lock's gun struck the wall above his head. Plaster dusted his black hair. He didn't try for fancy shooting, he just cut loose with the rifle. Its heavy .30-30 bullet with a full charge of powder behind it flattened one of Lock's fingers that was clutching the gun butt. Deflected upward by the metal gun grip, the bullet caught the tip of Lock's nose, a corner of the left eye. Sight of the ugly exit wound at the back of the skull caused Diana's eyes to roll back in her head. Her knees caved. She dangled in a dead faint from the heavy rope knotted at her waist and attached to the anvil.

"Hipp, get at Lassiter's back!" Rambert was shouting as he wheeled to seek protection at a corner of the house. He looked in vain for Hipp.

"Drop it, Rambert!" Lassiter ordered.

But Lassiter's shout went unheeded. Rambert made a desperate play, now trying to reach Diana. To use her as leverage as Hipp had done earlier with the knife at her throat.

As Rambert sprinted toward the bundle of blond hair and pale dress twisted about an inert body, he fired twice back at Lassiter. One bullet puckered window glass to Lassiter's right and the next one whanged off a metal corner of the grillework.

"Damn you, Lassiter!" Rambert yelled in frustration because Lassiter made a poor target, dodging, weaving along the house wall. He moved so quickly that Rambert had no chance for accurate shooting. Lassiter, teeth bared, hair and shoulders dusted from adobe chips and flaking whitewashed plaster, was closing in.

Still at a hard run, Rambert tried to avoid him and skidded to one knee, ripping cloth and flesh. Reaching out with his left hand he tried to seize Diana by an ankle and pull her close enough to use as a shield. But she had been tied too securely to the anvil. She didn't budge.

Rambert lost his hat. Strands of thin red hair sprang loose from pomade to dance about on his scalp like wire. Blood darkened the torn material where the right knee was out of his pants leg.

Rambert looked desperately for Lassiter, then suddenly realized that Lassiter had gotten beyond him. He tried to swing around, did manage to thumb off a shot. But it only ticked a corner of a roof tile as the rifle erupted. Rambert felt as if he had been smashed down by a load of bricks.

Into his line of vision Lassiter appeared, the lips twisted, the big rifle gripped in hands browned from the sun. Powder smoke trailed from the muzzle to spread across the yard, along the house wall, by the blacksmith shop with its tilted roof. Then everything faded for a moment. Rambert was aware of hoofbeats and thought it had to be Lassiter fleeing. Hipp must have frightened him off, he thought.

The young blond had revived and was screaming, "Don't kill him, Lassiter! Hasn't there already been enough of that?"

"He's past the trees," Lassiter said in disgust. "Only way I can get him now is to ride him down."

"Please don't. Please don't leave me, Lassiter." Rambert lifted his head. It seemed strangely heavy. So it was Deacon Hipp, the coward, who was getting away, not Lassiter. He saw that Lassiter had cut the young wife free of ropes, stood her on her feet. She was clinging to Lassiter.

Rambert then noticed that she looked in his direction. He wondered why she shuddered and turned her head. Why did sight of him lying on the ground seem so revolting? He decided it was time to finish Lassiter. What a way for Lassiter to die, he thought, with a pretty woman clinging to his neck. Tears ran down her fair cheeks and into the neckline of the dress.

Rambert closed the fingers of his right hand, believing he still gripped his weapon. But the fingers only curled against themselves. His gun was gone. He tried to think, then realized Lassiter must have taken it.

Then he realized it was sight of his own blood that had turned Diana pale. He could see it now, bubbling out of his chest. And he realized suddenly that there would be no more Belleville for him, no more pretty women.

"Lassiter, the money wasn't ever under the safe, was it?" Rambert heard himself say.

"I don't know where the hell it is. I hoped you'd spend an hour knocking holes in the floor to try and find out. But it wasn't necessary."

Lassiter started to say something else about the missing gold. But Rambert was silent now, staring skyward with empty eyes.

Bruce lurched from the house, his eyes frantic. He saw Brownie Lock's gun, stooped and picked it up. Since coming West the pink-cheeked adolescent look had gained a certain maturity. His face was browned from the sun.

"Are they gone?" he cried, running toward Lassiter who was reloading the rifle. Empty cartridges flipped onto the hard ground, brass casings gleaming in the sun. "I saw Hipp riding away like mad."

"He'll be back," Lassiter said grimly. "He's got a whiff of the gold."

Diana leaned against the anvil, looking as if she might faint again.

"It was awful, horrible." She shuddered.

"What happened before I got here?" he demanded in a low voice. "Did they rape you?"

Bruce overheard it and cried out before Diana could answer Lassiter's question. "How dare you use such a word to my wife?"

Lassiter looked at him. "I dare," he said thinly. "Because if they did, I won't feel one damn bit of regret for the ones I killed."

"They wouldn't dare!" Bruce said.

"You better grow up, Bruce," Lassiter said. He found his .44 in a tangle of shrubbery grown wild near the house, where Hipp had tossed it. "You've got a pretty wife," Lassiter continued. "You better start learning to protect her."

"I can take care of myself," Diana said in a weak voice.

Claire had come up from the office, her steps dragging. She stood looking at the dead sprawled in the yard. Lassiter had no idea how long she'd been standing there.

"You all right?" he asked her.

She nodded. "When I heard the shooting, I was scared something would happen to you."

"We're not out of it yet," he grunted. "Not by a damn sight."

Chapter Sixteen

Bruce put a hand on Diana's arm. "You still frightened?" he asked.

She looked at him, then at Lassiter who was entering the house. "Not as much as I was. I guess these last few days I've grown up all of a sudden."

"That Lassiter's quite a man."

"Yes, he certainly is." Diana looked down at a rope burn on her wrist. "I never met anyone quite like him." Lassiter surveyed the damage to the house. Holes had been smashed in the two inner walls of the bedroom formerly occupied by the late owner of OS ranch. One of the supporting walls in the hallway had been damaged. There were several holes in the floor, marked by pieces of broken tile and heaps of dirt. He dragged Sam Varney's body out across the veranda and to the front steps. He felt done in. He could taste gunsmoke. When he returned to the house, Claire followed him through the many rooms, her green eyes bitter. At last she said in despair, "They ruined my beautiful house."

Bruce entered the room, looking grim. "Not your house," he reminded. "I'm the heir. I guess I finally realize what you've been up to. Trying to sway me."

"Your grandfather promised everything to me."

"Verbal contracts are worthless," Bruce said, making a rueful gesture. "I realize most everyone out here thinks I'm brainless, but I do know a thing or two. In spite of what some people may think." He looked accusingly at Diana. They had been arguing again.

Diana had changed the dress that had been soiled and torn when she resisted being tied. The one she wore now was yellow. Her long hair was tied back with a matching ribbon. At that moment she looked about sixteen to Lassiter.

"Time I had a decent meal," Lassiter said, and started for the kitchen. Seeing Diana looking so young, so vulnerable, pricked him with guilt when he thought of their night together in the Tres Vidas Hotel. Oh, to hell with it, he told himself, and looked around the big kitchen.

Claire hurried in, plucked a red-checkered apron from an antler rack and tied it around her waist. "You've done all the fighting," she said. "I'll do the cooking." She turned to Diana who had slipped into the kitchen. "You can give me a hand."

Diana looked uncomfortable. "I don't know much about kitchens."

"Or other things," Claire said with a nasty laugh.

"I suppose Bruce has complained about my deficiencies!" Diana's eyes were bold, but the subject matter turned her face crimson. Claire's laughter only deepened the blush.

"I can teach Bruce a thing or two," Claire said, showing her teeth. "But not you. You're hopeless."

"Ladies, for God's sakes, we need food, not you two trying to whittle each other to pieces," Lassiter complained.

"Now that I know for sure that my husband has dallied with another woman," Diana said, chin lifted, "I shall return to New York and sue for divorce." Lassiter didn't laugh at her, but his sardonic smile told it all. While Claire was raising coals in the stove into flame, he whispered, "Better not hide behind a glass wall, Diana. Somebody might throw a brick."

Her eyes flashed and she drew back her hand as if to crack him across the face. But he caught her wrist. "Don't be so high and mighty," he advised in a low voice. "Give Bruce a chance. You two needed to sample life. And you have. Both of you." He looked at her meaningfully and she lowered her eyes.

"You like Claire, don't you?" she asked brokenly.

"I like you both."

She lifted her eyes; they were wet with tears. "My emotions are tearing me to pieces."

"You'd never be happy with me, in case that's the thought rolling around in your head. You've got a husband. I've got a widow in Mexico."

That shocked her. "Prettier than I am, I suppose," she finally managed.

Lassiter grinned. "About equal, I'd say." The banter eased his tension in this house of death. And he knew deep inside that before too many hours passed they could face more of it.

Claire found some steak and potatoes in the root cellar. She opened a tin of green beans and made gravy. Then she sent Bruce to fetch Lassiter, who had gone outside to take a look around.

Lassiter was staring at the lake when he heard the scuff of a bootheel at his back. He spun, the .44 in his hand, cocked pointed at the midriff of a surprised Bruce. Bruce seemed frozen in shock. As he holstered the gun, Lassiter said gruffly, "Next time sing out before you come up behind me. Makes me nervous. We've got some dead to bury. We'll need picks and shovels. You better give me a hand."

"Miss Manning says the food is on the table," Bruce said, his voice nearly normal. But he still hadn't regained all of his color.

"We'll do the burying later, then," Lassiter said.

Bruce couldn't get over seeing Lassiter move with such blinding speed. He fell in step with Lassiter. "I thought you were going to kill me."

"No reason to."

"Maybe to steal my wife," Bruce blurted.

"You forgot to dry yourself off behind the ears, kid."

That angered Bruce. "I don't have to take your insults on my own ranch."

"Another week of people like Hipp and you'll have nothing but pulverized adobe bricks. You won't even have a ranch."

"You belittle me—that's what I don't like. And I am suspicious of you and Diana, not to mention Ryan. Oh, he and Diana had a good story to tell—wanting to find my grandfather's treasure and surprise me with it."

Lassiter forced a scornful laugh. "You trying to act so noble while you and Claire do it right under your wife's nose."

"Miss Manning and I are friends only."

"Miss Manning. That what you call her in the bedroom?" Lassiter looked around at the shorter, younger man who was trying to match his stride. "You've got a nice wife. If Claire taught you anything, and I'm sure she did, remember it. And *use* it."

"I swear to God I don't understand the way you people out here live and talk. You speak of something so sacred with about as much feeling as you'd show buying wine."

"It's because life is short, Bruce. Damned short. And out here it can end awful sudden."

Bruce gave a long sigh. "After today I should realize that, I guess." His voice lost most of its truculence. "Three men dead." He shuddered. A late afternoon sun dipped below the cottonwoods on the far side of the lake.

Lassiter halted. "One of us better stand guard and keep watch for Hipp."

Bruce swallowed. "You really believe Hipp will be back?"

"Yeah. And I've got a hunch he won't be alone."

"I'll stand guard."

"Good. I was hoping you'd say that. I haven't had much in my stomach today. I need food." He clapped Bruce on the shoulder. "Can I count on you to keep your eyes open?"

"I won't fail you, Lassiter."

Lassiter nodded his approval and walked away. Young Redgate was learning that life in the West meant sacrifice.

In the house Lassiter told Diana that Bruce was acting as lookout. She said she'd wait and eat with him. Lassiter sat down, smiling to himself. Diana was showing promise.

After the meal, Lassiter got Claire aside. "Forget any ideas about getting Bruce to trade wives."

"I deserve this ranch." Her chin came up, the green eyes bright with anger. Lassiter agreed with her.

"Sure you deserve it. You put up with that old bastard and he shouldn't have lied to you. But don't make Bruce your ace in the hole. There'll be another way."

She gave a bitter laugh as she watched him spoon gravy over steak and potatoes. "You talking about the Redgate gold? Even I'm beginning to doubt that it even exists."

"I've become a believer. By God it *does* exist."

"But where?"

Lassiter looked around. Bruce was outside, Diana had gone to their room. "Think back, Claire," he urged. "Try and remember everything the old man told you.

He must have let *something* slip. He was getting senile, we both know that. Like the time he forgot to lock that Redgate gun up in the safe. And he didn't even seem to miss it, so you said."

Some of the old excitement returned to Claire's eyes. "Maybe the clue is in the gun. Maybe on the un derside of the gun grips."

He told her he'd taken the gun apart. "The gun grips are solid gold and so is the heel plate. But there's nothing underneath that would give a clue to the missing gold bullion."

Claire frowned, bit her lips. "Leland told me once that a fortuneteller said that gold would always pro tect him from danger. That was when he was a young man. He had two guns and a cavalry saber. Coated with black paint. But I had no idea they were gold And I guess they were, all right."

"Didn't the old bastard have any message for his grandson? He must have said something."

"Just that he hated him." Claire thought about it then said, "Funny, but I'm wondering if his hatred wa as deep as he liked to pretend."

"What makes you think so?"

"I don't know." She made a vague gesture. "Just a idea. Came to me all of a sudden."

"That's all he said? Just that he hated Bruce?"

"He did tell me to stay around because I'd probabl break up his grandson's marriage. He wanted Bruc to have nothing, so he claimed. Just an old house an some acreage, but no money and no cattle." Clai shook her head. "I guess he was worse than senil Just plain crazy."

"Maybe a little touched as they say," Lassiter sa thoughtfully, "but I've got a hunch he knew wh he was doing." He reached across the table to gr laire's hand. "Think back. Think about the gold. He nust have said *something*."

"All he kept saying over and over was that I was to ell his grandson to 'buy your gold.' And every time he aid it I tried to figure if I had heard it right. But it always ame out the same, even if it didn't make any sense."

"Hmmmm."

"There at the last his accent got so thick I could ıardly make out anything he said. Let alone 'buy our gold.'"

"Buy your gold," Lassiter mused, staring through doorway at one of the ruined walls. "If you've got old, there's no reason to buy it. And why *'your'* gold? f there's gold around here it's Redgate's gold. If the ıld man as Redgate was talking and he said 'buy ny gold,' it might make a little more sense. But not nuch." Suddenly Lassiter stiffened and swore softly. laire looked at him in surprise. "What is it?"

"Just happened to think of something."

"Something that would lead us to the money?" she lemanded eagerly.

Lassiter decided to mask his own excitement with ndifference. "Likely nothing at all," he said with a hrug. "But I'll think about it."

"Lassiter, *tell* me!"

"Later."

He walked away, found shovels and picks in a toolhed and shouted for Bruce to join him. They buried he dead out behind a barn and at the same time kept ın eye peeled for riders.

Chapter Seventeen

When Lassiter came off the night watch Claire p
sisted in her attempts to get Lassiter to reveal what
had in mind about the missing gold. But all he wo
say was, "Later."

The whole thing was tricky enough as it was w
a virtual tenderfoot to side him, plus two young
dies. He might be able to count on Claire; at least
wouldn't panic at the sound of gunfire. Diana Redg
might summon up a little courage but likely wo
crumble if faced with real danger.

What he needed now was sleep. He'd been up
night, not trusting Bruce to stay awake and sou
the alarm if trouble developed. *When* it develop
was more to the point, he reflected wearily, becau
it was inevitable.

So far, there was only Hipp to contend with a
what hardcases he could round up to help him fin
the job. And Tarsh of course would make his own
for the gold. But when?

It was barely dawn when Lassiter went to bed.
slept till noon.

In a matter of hours, a few days at the most, the sto
of the Redgate gold would spread like a kerosene-
fire through dry grass. Not the old myth with the
tendant spurious treasure maps, but solid evidence t
a Nevada gold mine had been looted and a fortune
gold ingots brought into the area of the Furnace at
close of the Civil War. And then it had simply vanish

along with a colonel, eight men, and a mule train. Nine men, so the blind guitaron player had told Lassiter that day at Belleville. That was when Abran assumed Colonel Redgate had perished along with others in the party of Southern sympathizers in an attempt to rush gold to the Confederacy to keep Lee's army in the field through that final summer of hostilities.

But Colonel Redgate had survived, Lassiter knew now. Ormsby and Redgate were one and the same. Had the colonel, knowing the war was lost, somehow contrived to murder the others in his party? Or had the others died in the windstorm that had ravaged the Furnace that year, according to old-timers.

No matter how the others had perished, the fact remained that the colonel had somehow built a mansion, stocked a ranch, dammed a stream to form his own "bayou," and done it all without anyone realizing his true identity.

According to Abran, the area had been sparsely populated if at all at that time. No matter how the colonel had built his empire, there was no denying that it had been done. Lassiter had to give the old man credit for superb planning. How many men had disappeared over the years who might have inadvertently stumbled onto the secret, no one would ever know.

In talking with Bruce, Lassiter had the feeling the colonel's mind had started to come apart eleven years ago. He had counted on his grandson, aged ten, to change his name to Ormsby and live with him at the ranch. But old hatred over the Civil War had practically turned the colonel into a recluse. Leland Ormsby-Redgate had seldom visited Tres Vidas and only a few times had he gone north to Santa Rita.

Shortly past noon Claire cooked Lassiter a breakfast of tough steak and leftover beans. She leaned against

the work table, wearing her checkered apron, ar
crossed over her breasts. She watched him eat, looki
worried.

"Any plans, Lassiter?" she asked when he had f
ished the last of the coffee.

He was noncommittal. "Got a couple rolling arou
in my head," was all he said.

"Also rolling around in your head is some ic
where the gold is." She came over and placed h
hands on the table and leaned down. He could ca
her scent and the warmth of her body through t
black dress she was wearing that day. It revealed eve
curve and ripple, which made him wonder if she wo
the dress only to bedevil Diana and catch the eye
her young husband. "You can't fool me, Lassiter," s
hissed. "Let's us get it and clear out before Bruce a
that fragile doll of his know what happened."

Lassiter set down the empty cup and shook
head. There was a faint smell of crumbled adobe fro
the smashed walls. "Wouldn't be right to run out
them," he said flatly.

"Damn it, if Leland was really Colonel Redga
then I deserve all the gold." Her green eyes flashed
earned it, God knows."

"So you've said. Some gals get five dollars a tri
Some do it for a dollar. You did it for a ranch."

She lifted a threatening hand. "I should slap yo
face."

"Don't try it." He leaned back in his chair a
looked at her coldly. "No matter what you think of t
Redgates, they deserve a share."

"It should be mine. Every ounce of that gold. Mine

"Don't get yourself so riled up or you'll bust yo
corset strings."

"I don't wear a corset."

"Yeah, I remember." He gave her a hard grin.

"Of course I intend for you to share the gold with me."

"How nice."

"Don't be so smug. Dammit, Lassiter, we're a good team in bed or out of it. With the gold we could go to South America. I'd be your duchess."

"Who put that idea in your head? Joe Tarsh?"

She looked down at her nails. "I hate Joe Tarsh." She backed away from the table, her spine stiff. "I don't understand you. We don't need anyone else. Just us. Isn't that what we've always wanted, from the first?"

A familiar sardonic smile slid across his lips. "With Harry Benbow and Joe Tarsh in between."

"Benbow didn't count."

"Tarsh?" He waited while she looked away, stony-eyed.

He laughed at her. "Hell, admit it. Who cares? I know damn well Tarsh didn't get you so worked up you'd visit him at the Fortress just by holding your hand."

"You told me yourself that what's past is past and that only the present counts."

"Bravo."

"Don't use that word." She shuddered. "Leland was always using it."

"At least I got you to admit you weren't exactly faithful while I was away," he said in an amused voice.

"Nor were you with that tar-eyed senorita."

"A widow, not a senorita. And her eyes aren't black like tar. Black like olives."

"You're laughing at me and I don't like it. Like you did that day when I tried to tell you about the Redgate gold."

He walked out of the big kitchen and along a hallway, stepping over piles of broken adobe bricks. A dark

smear on the floor marked the spot where Sam Varn
had died.

Diana was at one of the narrow windows, lookin
indignant. "Did you see that disgusting dress Clai
is wearing?"

"More to the point, where's your husband?"
snapped.

"Where you told him to be. Outside with a rifle
When he started away she gripped his forearm wi
her two hands. They were slender hands, the na
pink. He looked down at them, remembering th
night in the hotel when timidity finally melted an
the fingertips delighted in their explorations of pr
viously forbidden territory. She spoke hoarsely. "I'
afraid, Lassiter. Seeing Bruce with a gun makes th
nightmare all so real."

"He's got a wife to support—and a ranch."

"Can't we get away from here? Come with us
Virginia City."

"Along with Gil Ryan, I suppose."

She shook her head. "I realize my responsibility
to Bruce. In fact we enjoy each other now. This mor
ing we—"

"This morning?" he interrupted.

A faint flush started at her earlobes and sprea
across the soft cheeks. "Lassiter, why are you lookin
at me like that?"

"No reason," he said coldly.

She seemed bewildered. "But I thought that's wh
you wanted. For Bruce and I to find pleasure in o
marriage."

She watched him put the rifle on a table and start
clean it. She said, "Aren't you going to relieve Bruce?

"Another hour won't matter."

"He's dead tired."

"Likely," Lassiter grunted as he worked with cleaning rag and gun oil. Diana cast him a worried glance and went to another part of the house.

Finally Lassiter went outside, carrying the rifle. Bruce was on the veranda, leaning against the rail, yawning. "I thought you'd never come, Lassiter," he said straightening up.

"Clean your rifle before you take a nap."

"But why? I need sleep. These last days I've had so little."

"It's your punishment," Lassiter said in a hard voice.

"Cleaning the rifle?" Bruce's mouth dropped open. "What did I *do*, for God's sake?"

"Diana said you enjoyed each other. *This morning*." Lassiter's dark eyes bored into Bruce's face. It began to redden as his wife's had in the house. "I don't give a damn what you did together," Lassiter snapped. "But you were supposed to be guarding this house from five o'clock till noon. And there's no way that can be done and at the same time enjoy a woman. In this case your wife."

Bruce hung his head. "All right, I was wrong. But we got to talking and—"

"Listen to me, Bruce. Once word is out about your grandfather's gold, there'll be so many hombres trying to dig for it that this ranch will look like the California Gold Rush." Lassiter punched the younger man lightly on the shoulder. "We don't have much time. Go get some shuteye and then we'll have a talk."

"I better go clean my rifle first."

"Do it later."

Lassiter had business of his own. He asked Diana to keep watch from the veranda and to yell if she saw anyone.

There were three sheds on the property. He hoped he would find what he was looking for in the first shed. But in this one there were only rusted ranch tools and cobwebs.

Claire came out of the house, no longer wearing the apron. A faint breeze flattened the black dress against her body. A splendidly built female, he had to admit. He was almost tempted; behind the shed they would be out of sight of the house. But he couldn't risk taking the time.

Claire's green eyes were excited. "You think the gold's in one of the sheds?"

He shook his head.

"Then what're you hunting for?" she demanded suspiciously.

He debated the wisdom of confiding in her, then decided she'd know about it anyway, sooner or later.

"Tarsh said there was dynamite in one of the sheds."

She looked at him in surprise. "Dynamite? Why do you want dynamite?"

"Tell you later." He went on with his search.

Chapter Eighteen

Deacon Hipp slept on the hard ground all night, then rode on to Tres Vidas. He was just entering town when he saw Sheriff Ernie Joplin and six or seven men riding in from the south. They were covered with dust and their horses looked about done in. It had been a year for desert winds. Not even the old-timers could remember another year quite like this one.

Joplin's jowls and roll of fat at his neck glistened with sweat. There were patches of it on his blue shirt. Hipp quickly ducked his horse between buildings before he was spotted. His heart pounded as he swung down. He was so close to the sheriff and his men that he could hear the creak of gun harness as they dismounted.

Joplin was saying in his booming voice, "Let's get a drink an' some eats. I'm hungry enough to eat half a cow all by myself. Chasin' them bastards clear to the border—I'm too old an' creaky for that kinda work. Anyhow, it was Tighe's job, not mine. His damn prison."

"Tighe won't be chasin' nobody," one of the men put in with a sour laugh.

A gaunt woman stepped from the Tres Vidas Store that she and her husband operated. She also took care of the demented OS rider, Mike Barlow.

"Mornin' Margaret," the sheriff called to her. He muttered under his breath, "Now what? I s'pose she wants me to chain up Barlow an' cart him up to the madhouse. What is it, Margaret?" he asked, smiling and removing his hat.

"Thought you'd like to know there's some fellas come in on the stage last night," she said, her narrow face flushed with excitement. "From Virginia City, they is."

"Don't say." The possemen had entered the cantina. Joplin thought longingly of Emilio Ruiz's good whiskey.

"Fellas is down here on account of Colonel Redgate swindlin' them an' some of their ancestors outa gold."

"I already talked to some of 'em, Margaret, up at the county seat an' said I'd look into it. But we had a prison breakout."

"There's a newspaper fella named Ryan who's with 'em. He's got a busted arm. Looks kinda suspicious to me, all them fellas claimin' that old man Ormsby was Colonel Redgate. Can you believe that, Ernie?"

"After what I've heard about Beeler an' his brother-in-law at the Fortress I'll believe 'most anything."

"Ryan an' them stockholders wants to talk to you, Ernie. Soon's I seen you ride in, they says."

Joplin cut her off with a weary wave of the hand. "Lead me to 'em, Margaret."

"I let 'em have the store for a meetin' hall. They're inside."

Deacon Hipp had overheard most of it while crouched in the alley, a hand over the snout of his horse so it wouldn't neigh. Hipp's long face with its heavy jaw betrayed excitement. Gold. Redgate's gold! He had come to town to try and find some hardcases to help him look for it; there were usually a few hanging around Tres Vidas. And before he could hunt for any the sheriff and his men had ridden in.

Hipp was trying to think what to do when he heard someone call his name. He stiffened and looked over his horse and into the hard blue eyes of Joe Tarsh.

"Deacon," Tarsh hissed. "You see the sheriff?"

"I ain't blind. Wish I was. Seein' that big bastard puts a lump of cold rock in my guts."

Tarsh came closer. "You wanta team up?"

Hipp cocked a suspicious eye at the big blond man. "For why?"

"The gold, damn it," Tarsh said in a low, tense voice. "It's somewheres out at OS. All of a sudden I got a strong feelin' about it."

Hipp nodded, saying he agreed. "That damn Lassiter gunned down everybody but me." He gave a few pertinent facts and then Tarsh grinned so fiercely that the ends of his pale mustache twitched.

"Lassiter's led a charmed life," he whispered. "But it's about to run dry."

"You figure the two of us can do it alone?"

"I got three men. Soon's I seen you ride in I says to myself, there's a fourth."

Hipp rubbed a hand over his hard jaw, met Tarsh's eyes, and read his mind. An unspoken agreement passed between them. Once the gold was found, it would be split only two ways. Those of the three who managed to survive the fight Lassiter was sure to put up would die kicking their boot-toes into the ground, wondering what had blown their backbones apart.

"Let's go," Hipp said quietly.

They led their horses out behind the livery barn and away from the buzzy of voices they could hear coming from the Tres Vidas Store.

Once in the saddle, Tarsh gave Hipp a confident grin and introduced the trio he'd rounded up just prior to Sheriff Joplin's appearance in town with a posse.

"This here's Deacon Hipp. Barney Sage, Luke Whipple, and Jay Cross." The men nodded, gestured a greeting but did not bother to shake hands.

Barney Sage had a face that someone once had worked over with a knife, leaving scars on forehead, each cheek and down the jawbone. "Tarsh says there's women out at OS," he said.

Whipple was tall and lank, with an Adam's apple big as a walnut. "Gold first. Women later." He winked at Jay Cross who was riding at his side.

Cross wore a fringed buckskin shirt taken from the body of a Cheyenne he'd killed for his horse and his squaw up on the Yellowstone. "Don't matter none to me which comes first," he said, giving the wink back to Whipple.

The trio had been chased out of Mexico when rurales began a roundup of rustlers, and were on their way north. Tarsh had worked with them before.

Hipp turned his head, revealed his tombstone teeth to Tarsh. "I aim to dab my rope on that blond. That's after I get through geldin' that lah-dee-dah husband of hers."

All the men laughed.

Tarsh kept his thoughts to himself. In Tres Vidas he had purchased shells for the .45 Lassiter had turned over to him, that had belonged to the late captain of prison guards. Besides having five loads in the gun, his pockets bulged with another two dozen. He intended, after Sage and Whipple and Cross were out of it, to save one special bullet for the back of Deacon Hipp's elongated skull.

Hipp said, "You mind sharin' that goodlookin' Claire with the rest of the boys?"

"We're partner, ain't we?" Tarsh laughed, but the slits of his eyes revealed a hardness as solid as the walls of the Redgate cave at the edge of the Furnace.

Had Bruce Redgate used the name of Ormsby as his grandfather stipulated, much bitterness, hatred and violent death might have been avoided. But on the way West he saw no harm in using Redgate for the last time.

By opening his mouth in Virginia City Bruce had dropped a stone into a pool and stirred the waters.

Gil Ryan had related the story to Harry Benbow, who immediately went off on his own to try and trace the missing bullion from the Empire Mine. But pressure made him drink and that made him think of his young and pretty wife who had run away with a twenty-year-old farrier who worked for a stage line.

Harry Benbow with his experience as a detective, had the best chance of anyone of either proving the story of Redgate gold to be a myth, which most everyone believed, or in fact a reality.

But the stone Bruce had dropped into the pool was still making ever widening circles. Gil Ryan had feverishly thrown himself into the business of rounding up former stockholders of the defunct Empire Mine. There were only two original stockholders, but three descendants, including Gil Ryan.

In the rear of the Tres Vidas Store Sheriff Ernie Joplin tried not to show his weariness to these important people and listened politely.

As he had told some of them at the county seat earlier in the month, he believed the story of the Redgate gold to be pure fabrication, and if he ever caught the maker of Redgate maps on the U.S. side of the line he'd see him thrown into the Fortress for twenty years.

Whereupon Gil Ryan slid off a counter where he had been sitting and produced what he called proof. It was in the form of old letters, of stock certificates one of the stockholders had brought with him from Nevada. There were also news clippings from Carson City and Virginia City papers of the time.

And there was a daguerrotype of Colonel Redgate, bearded and erect in the butternut of a Southern colonel. At his belt was a saber and two large pistols, possibly Remingtons.

"Sheriff, cover the beard and see what you have," Ryan said excitedly.

Joplin placed a piece of paper over the lower half of the face and the eyes of Leland Ormsby of OS ranch looked out at him.

"You mean there really is a million dollars in gold?"

"At least that much," Ryan said with a triumphant smile.

"Sonofabitch," the sheriff muttered and stared unseeing at some bolts of muslin on one of the store counters.

Lassiter squatted on his heels and peered through a maze of spiderwebs at the two wooden boxes. The larger one contained sticks of dynamite, according to the lettering on the side, the smaller one caps.

He straightened up, trying to remember all he had heard about dynamite. It was tricky to handle when it got old, so he remembered someone telling him. But how long had this stuff been in the shed? Since some of it had been planted to seal off the entrance to old Leland Ormsby-Redgate's sepulcher. And how long ago was that? Tarsh might know, but to hell with him.

Before he could find Tarsh, even if he wanted to, the gold-seekers would be swarming across OS ranch.

Bruce Redgate came to the shed, waving a paper in the air. "All signed," he cried in his excitement. "You really know where it's hidden?"

Lassiter took the paper without answer. An hour ago he had called a meeting. As Diana had the best handwriting she was instructed to make four copies of an agreement. If the Redgate gold was found, Bruce was to receive a full share, his wife a full share. The other two shares would go to Claire and Lassiter. Lassiter had already affixed his signature to the other copies, then come to the yard to continue his search for the dynamite. He folded the copy Bruce had given him and shoved it into his pocket; it had been signed by the other three participants.

Bruce saw the dynamite for the first time. "So this is what you've been hunting for."

Lassiter got a sour look on his face. "I pawed through two sheds. It would have to be in the last one."

"Do you plan to blow up the house?" Bruce asked in amazement.

"I'm halfway afraid if I try to move the dynamite, I'll be the one blown up," he said without answering Bruce's question.

"I hate to see the house destroyed," Bruce said wistfully. He looked back at the rambling adobe mansion his grandfather had built back in the '60s. White wash had peeled off the walls and some of the roof tiles were missing or askew. There were scars on the walls where bullets had gouged out chunks of adobe. Several windows had been drilled or knocked out by bullets. And some of the interior had been smashed by a sledge hammer. "It's the only thing I have left," Bruce went on, his voice breaking, "of my family."

"Cheer up. If we find the gold you can build a dozen houses." He wanted to get rid of Bruce till he carefully thought out his next moves. He pointed at the far pasture out beyond the last barn. "Why don't you take a look out there? If you see anything, yell."

Claire came up from the house, still wearing the black dress the old man had bought her out of a catalogue. It shimmered in the sunlight. "So you found it, the dynamite," she said, looking into the shed.

Gingerly he pried open the lid of the box containing the sticks of dynamite. He pushed the lid aside and got out half a dozen sticks. The palms of his hands turned cold when he gathered up caps and fuses and put everything carefully into the saddlebags of the hors he had kept saddled for emergencies.

Claire tugged at his shirt sleeve. "Where's the gold? she gasped. "Where *is* it?"

Lassiter's smile was thin. He decided she might a well know. "Remember the old man telling you to giv a message to his grandson? Buy your gold?"

"He said it over and over. It makes no sense."

"With that molasses accent of his it sounded lik 'buy your gold.' But I've got a hunch what he reall meant was *bayou gold*."

"That doesn't make any more sense than the oth er—" Then her mouth popped open and her gree eyes got big. "He always called that lake his bayou."

"I aim to blow up that dam. And drain the lake!"

"Oh, my God, do you really think it's *there*?"

"Bruce said that when he came out here as a kid the old man told him that there was a big dry was where the lake is now. I got a feeling that's wher the whole party, mules and gold, got trapped in tha sandstorm. The old man covered it up with his lake Go on back to the house and stay put till I get finishe with my business," he said.

She eyes him suspiciously. "And you'll take the gol for yourself."

He gave her a shove. "Go ahead to the house Trust me."

She seemed torn, nibbling her lower lip with he teeth, but finally she walked off.

Bruce came walking around a comer of the bar just as Lassiter got a shovel and pick out of one of th sheds. "I didn't see a thing out there," he reported.

Just as Lassiter was ready to mount up, he heard someone running. He looked around. Diana came a a dead run out of the cottonwoods behind the house

Her hair had come loose from its pins and spilled about her frightened face.

"There's a horseman coming!" she cried.

"He alone?" Lassiter demanded, running, rifle swinging from a long arm.

"I didn't see anybody with him," Diana said, fighting for breath after her run.

"What's he look like?"

"Big and he looks like that man who had the rifle that you shot—"

"Tarsh!" Lassiter snapped.

Lassiter gripped Diana by the arm and bounded with her around a corner of the house. He saw no sign of movement out on the flats. But he shaded his eyes, tried a second time, shifting his gaze toward the trees that had been planted as a windbreak on the far side of the lake.

"Where'd you last see him?" he demanded so harshly that Diana jumped. She pointed toward the edge of the Furnace. "Over there, Lassiter!"

Lassiter squinted at clumps of buckbrush and cholla and boulders, some nearly large enough to hide a man on a horse. But there was no sign of Tarsh.

"He made a move while you came to get me," Lassiter said through his teeth. Lassiter was sorry she hadn't screamed a warning, so he would know something was up. Instead she had taken her eyes off the approaching rider just long enough for Tarsh to reach cover. But where? And just where the hell was Claire?

Then he saw her step to the veranda. He went to her and said, "Tarsh is out there somewhere!" He watched for a reaction but all he saw was a tightening of her lips.

"Don't let that old love light make you careless where Tarsh's concerned," he warned.

Her green eyes snapped. "That love light went out weeks ago. What are you going to do now?"

"Like I said, take a chance on that dynamite. You keep your mouth shut about what I told you."

She nodded. "Please be careful."

But he was gone. He cornered Bruce and ordered him to stand guard with the rifle. "You see anybody heading this way, warn them off. If they won't listen, shoot!"

Bruce licked his lips and nodded that he understood.

Making sure he had matches, Lassiter put shovel and pick under an arm and mounted up. He rode away from the house, keeping to the tree wherever possible. He kept his horse at a careful walk because of the dynamite. It crossed his mind that if Tarsh decided to try for a shot, it might hit one of the caps and set off the dynamite in the saddlebags. If so there wouldn't be much left of him and the horse but a smear.

Chapter Nineteen

Tarsh had had his look at the house and now rode back to where the others waited. They were in a gully deep enough to screen them from anyone at the house or riding along the ranch road. Tarsh had gone ahead to scout around because it was agreed that he knew more about the OS ranch than any of the rest of them.

Hipp stood spradled-legged, jaw outthrust. "What'd you see?"

"Nothin' but that cute Redgate female."

"That's for me," Deacon Hipp said, rubbing his long hands together. "See anybody else?"

"No sign of Lassiter," Tarsh admitted. "That gal bein' on the porch instead of her husband or Lassiter kinda worries me."

"Why?" Hipp demanded.

"Got a wolf-trap smell about it. I don't aim to get my hind leg caught in it."

"What you figure we should do?" Hipp asked narrowly.

"Wait till dark."

Jay Cross was leaning against the bank of the dry wash. Some sand spilled down from above and dusted the shoulders of his buckskin shirt. "You worried about us against Lassiter an' that kid an' a coupla wimmen?"

"Jay's right," Whipple put in, the oversize Adam's apple twitching. "Let's got get 'em *now*."

Barney Sage had been seated. He got up, brushed sand from the seat of worn canvas pants, the scarred face turned to Whipple. "We better listen to Tarsh."

"Waitin' ain't for me!" Cross said thinly. "Hell, we can do it in broad daylight."

Hipp shook his head. "Tarsh, whyn't you go have another look? Just make stare that goddamn Lassiter ain't got some friends. He's had time to corral a few since I seen him last."

"Might be a good idea," Tarsh agreed. He mounted up, gave a short laugh, and slapped the butt of the .45 that had belonged to Beeler. "Just might be I could get Lassiter in my sights."

And Tarsh thought: He made me crawl more'n once. He won't again.

Lassiter studied the dam. Over the years the two clay pipes, each a foot in diameter, that had acted as a spillway over the years, had gradually deteriorated. Water had seeped down into the stones and earth of the dam. He stood there, trying to figure out the best place to place the dynamite. A large rock two feet or so below the surface of the soggy rock and earthen dam caught his eye. He got the pick and, leaning over, sank its point, loosening the rock.

As he stood there, bracing his feet on the uneven lip of the dam, he thought of some of the things he would do with the money. Among them, buying a pair of fine saddle horses to be sent anonymously to a rancher named Bartlett, replacements for the pair Tarsh had stolen on the night of the mason break.

As he lifted the pick for another dig at the rock, he heard a horse coming from the house. It was Claire in riding clothes, black hair flying. Lassiter swore under his breath and tried to wave her back.

But it did no good. She came on, swinging down on the far side of the twenty-foot dam. She started across the dam. "I've just got to see if you're right, Lassiter. I've just *got* to!"

Holding the pick in one hand, he tried to grab her arm with the other. But she jumped back, causing him to come close to losing his balance and tumbling down the twelve-foot face of the dam.

"Get back to the house!" he shouted. "If Tarsh is really hanging around here—"

"I'm sure he wouldn't hurt me," she said, her eyes defiant.

"You told me once you didn't trust him," he reminded, hoping to keep her interest so he could get in close enough to get her away from the dynamite which he had placed on the lip of the dam only a foot or so from where she was standing.

"That's beside the point. I've got a right to see that gold."

"Me too," came a rough male voice at Lassiter's back.

"Joe!" Claire cried, a hand flying to her mouth.

Lassiter turned carefully to look over his shoulder. Tarsh was afoot, grinning at him. He had found a hat and it was pulled low over the yellow brows. His teeth showed through the straggly pale mustache.

He held a gun. It looked like Beeler's .45, the hammer eared back. Tarsh had evidently left his horse some distance away and sneaked up through the cottonwoods.

Lassiter pointed the pick at the dynamite and caps and fuse that had been placed at the edge of the dam. "A stray bullet lands in there and we're all of us goners."

"I won't be so damn careless as all that," Tarsh said. He laughed, then the lips lost their curve and he looked at Lassiter, then at the dynamite and at the water beginning to gush from around the loosened rock. "You figure the gold's in the lake, don't you?"

"Yeah, Tarsh, that's how I figure it!" Lassiter had turned slowly on the lip of the dam, holding the pick.

Claire stood rigid, hand still held at her mouth as if frozen against the white teeth.

"I could give a shout," Tarsh said. "Hipp an' three of my amigos are less'n a quarter of a mile away." Lassiter wasn't surprised. He probably should have waited, had a showdown first, then gone after the gold later. But he had worried that someone else might get the same idea and beat him to the treasure. Lassiter wondered if he could shift his grip to the end of the pick handle, swing it in a wide enough arc that would drive the metal point into Tarsh's flesh.

"Sure you could give a shout," Lassiter agreed, inching forward, not taking his eyes from Tarsh's face and at the same time making sure of his footing. "But you'd like the gold for yourself and leave them out of it."

"Mebby me an' you after all, compadre," Tarsh said, the old cocky grin twisting his mouth ends up into the mustache. "Blow that dam an' you'll catch Hipp an' the others. They're in the wash that's the old creek bed."

"Haven't time to blow it," Lassiter said. He couldn't reach Tarsh, but he could reach the rock. Taking the pick in both hands he sank its point into the ooze of mud forming around the rock. It loosened even more. Water began to pour out. Tarsh watched in fascination as the rock popped like a cannon ball and went rolling down the slant and along the twisting five foot gully the old creek had cut through desert sand over the centuries. Lassiter pretended to watch it bounding away.

And as a great spout of water erupted, he leaped for Tarsh. Tarsh's eyes had been riveted on the crumbling dam. At the last moment he realized what Lassiter was up to. He jumped back just as Lassiter swung the pick. Tarsh's scream was an unearthly sound as the point of the pick ripped the upper left arm. Blood spurted.

Tarsh fired the gun as he lost balance, Lassiter ramming the butt end of the pick into his face. The impact made the shot go wild. But it was close enough so that Lassiter felt a twitching at the crown of his black hat. Tarsh was down, unmoving.

As the water poured through the rapidly widening rift in the dam and turned into a roaring torrent, Lassiter had to fling the pick aside. He leaped for the far side of the crumbling dam where Claire stood as if transfixed.

Their two horses, despite the trailed reins, danced and pivoted in terror. Water pouring down into the stream-bed sounded like a cannonade. It swept the dynamite along the streambed in a great flood of water and froth that ate into the sand banks, and started them crumbling.

Lassiter seized the reins of the two horses, shoved Claire toward her own. "Get out! " he yelled above the roar of water.

Claire cried, "Joe, *don't*!"

Lassiter whipped around. He had thought Tarsh to be out of it, at least for now. But he wasn't. Tarsh had staggered to his feet. His face had been ruined by the blunt end of the pick. In that shattered part of a second, Tarsh's lips twisted in pain and rage as he leveled the cocked .45.

It was instinct that saved Lassiter. He jerked aside, the .45 spitting. Tarsh was knocked flat, the left side of the neck already a bubbling redness. Lassiter felt a little sick, but only for an instant. At one time he had almost liked Joe Tarsh. He hadn't particularly enjoyed killing him. But it had been inevitable from the first.

Hardly more than a minute had elapsed since the first water shot through the hole in the dam and Tarsh had made his play. Now the torrent surged and thundered, the last of the dam completely gone. Rocks and mud went flying. Banks of the lake were crumbling, widening the gap where the dam had been only a short time before.

***

A quarter of a mile or so down the twisting gully, the roaring had alerted the four men there. As the ground began to shake, Hipp was first in the saddle, yelling wildly. He jumped his horse up the sand bank and behind him came Jay Cross, then the scar-faced Barney Sage.

Whipple reacted too slowly. With one foot in the stirrup he saw the wall of water and flung an arm across his face as if that would protect him from the savage flood. And then the wall of water smashed into him. His horse, the whites of its eyes showing, was swept away, Whipple clinging to the mane. Down the gully the flood raced, spilled over banks, and near the road spindly cottonwoods were jerked out by the roots. And at the road itself the plank bridge disintegrated as if smashed by a giant's boot. Whipple disappeared among the timbers.

As quickly as it had come, the torrent began to diminish, bubbling and spreading out over the flats, the main body surging into its natural underground passage. In minutes it would all be gone, flowing somewhere deep under the Furnace.

And the lake itself, no more than five feet in depth at the deepest point, was only a great muddied depression in the earth, originally hollowed out over the centuries by the elements, then filled with water from a dammed up creek. All done by a colonel of the defeated South who was also a thief who had stripped a mine of gold bullion, causing it to go under.

And stirred by the churning mud as the dam collapsed, were gleaming bones—the rib cage of a mule. And of a human. And another and another. Meeting the sun again after years of darkness.

Gleaming faintly yellow where roiling waters had stripped away a coating of grime, upended in the mud, was a gold ingot.

***

Lassiter had no time to reload, only to spur the horse, for he saw the riders swarming in on the house at a gallop. Three of them. He recognized Deacon Hipp, bent over in the saddle, lank hair blowing from under a dusty hat, a long-barreled pistol gripped in his hand.

Diana was on the veranda. She had stared in horror as she watched the lake sucked out where the dam had been, like water gushing from a bucket when the rusted bottom suddenly gives way.

She saw the blond man in the distance shot down by Lassiter. She saw Lassiter approaching the house at a gallop, and far behind was Claire.

But closer in were others. Her face went dead white as she recognized Deacon Hipp who had held a knife to her throat.

She screamed, knees nearly buckling in her sudden fear. She held a rifle in trembling hands, but could not lift it. She stood frozen in her terror as the first of the riders reached the veranda.

He was a fierce looking man wearing a buckskin shirt he had taken from a dead Cheyenne after murdering his woman. Jay Cross leaped off his horse and toward Diana, waving a gun at her frightened face.

Bruce Redgate, bounding from the house with a rifle, fired blindly. Mingled with the roar of the gun, the swirl of powdersmoke, was the savage scream Jay Cross uttered prior to the moment of death.

Bruce looked ill as he stared at the man he had killed. Then he thrust Diana behind him and waited for the next of the riders to try and take his wife. In his inexperience and fright he forgot to lever a fresh shell into the breech.

But by then Hipp, storming toward the house, had seen Lassiter coming. He veered on the racing pony and shouted at Barney Sage above the roar of hoofs.

"Behind you, Sage! It's *Lassiter*!"

Lassiter picked the nearest target as Sage twisted in the saddle and tried to shoot him off the back of his speeding horse. Sage's scarred face collapsed as a bullet from the .44 smashed the breastbone at a level with the heart.

In the yelling and gunfire, the snorts of the horses, the pound of hooves, Hipp made a flying leap from the saddle. He cleared the veranda wall and dropped lightly onto the tiles. Bruce was dragging an unconscious Diana toward the house. Hipp lunged past the body of Cross, sprawled on the veranda in a widening pool of blood.

Hipp flung himself toward the girl and seized her by an ankle. Bruce swung the rifle at his head. Hipp shot him. Bruce sat down on the veranda, an odd look on his face. Then he fell flat as Diana sat up and looked in horror at the blood on the left side of Bruce's shirt. Lassiter closed in.

"Hipp!"

Lassiter shouted and took the veranda steps two at a time. Deacon Hipp swung around, pulling aside the pistol he had aimed at Bruce Redgate's head, aiming it instead at Lassiter.

They fired simultaneously. Lassiter twisted aside, but felt a burning sensation along his ribs. Deacon Hipp's tombstone front teeth disappeared into the dark cavern of his mouth, taken out by the bullet that ripped apart the back of his skull.

After ascertaining that Bruce's wound was superficial, Lassiter slipped away. His ribs burned like fire where Hipp's bullet had burned him, but he had no time to worry about it. He rode back to the lake. Miraculously the ax was wedged against a tree trunk where the outpouring of water had swept across level ground. He worked swiftly, dripping with mud.

Far back in the trees he used the ax to dig a hole. Quickly he dropped in five of the gold ingots, was going back for more when he heard a body of riders approaching. He hastily covered the ingots, threw a matting of dried leaves over the fresh dirt, then clambered back down into the lake bed just as Sheriff Ernie Joplin and his posse rode up. Behind them were several well-dressed men, looking a little frightened. Gil Ryan, his arm still in a sling, was in this latter group.

"The gold," Lassiter panted. "All here. I made sure."

Joplin looked at the muddied figure, dismounted and had his own close look. Then he and the possemen and the stockholders of Empire Mine also mucked around, dredging up ingots.

They washed the gold in the stream that now flowed freely, no longer dammed. The gold, without its coating of mud, gleamed in the late afternoon sunshine.

"It was Bruce Redgate figured out where the gold had been hidden all these years," Lassiter said later after the gold had been transported to the house in a ranch wagon.

Bruce, his shoulder bandaged, sat in one of the big Spanish chairs. He started to open his mouth, but Lassiter waved him to silence and continued telling the stockholders that they owed recovery of the fortune to one man only, Bruce Redgate.

"He and his wife should get equal shares," Lassiter finished. He looked around at the many faces. It was the sheriff who agreed that Lassiter was right.

"But what about me?" Claire whispered anxiously.

Lassiter leaned over and said something quietly. She relaxed and looked happy.

Later, after they had eaten and the dead had been buried, Sheriff Joplin got Lassiter aside. "I got a hunch it's you smelled out that gold. Young Redgate ain't got the brains for it. And you, you scoundrel, I oughta jail you for bustin' outa the Fortress. But—" He punched Lassiter lightly on the arm and walked away.

That night Lassiter and Claire went to the Tres Vidas Hotel. He had his old room, the one he and Diana Redgate had shared.

Claire, her long body gleaming in the lamplight, said, "Do you realize it's the first time we've shared a real bed?"

"Better than the grass on the backside of what used to be the lake."

"Diana looked sad when you said you weren't coming back "

"Your imagination," he said with a shrug. She and Bruce would be all right; Joplin had promised to find them a good man to help run the ranch.

Claire played with Lassiter's chest hair and said, "When do we dig up our share of the gold, honey?"

"Tomorrow. One gold brick for you, four for me."

"Why not share equal?" she demanded.

"Because I'm using my share to buy back a rancho for a young widow I know. If it hadn't been for her late husband, I'd be long dead. And you wouldn't even have a smell of that gold."

She sulked for a time, but had to be satisfied with her good fortune. She was more than satisfied with Lassiter himself.

That night Lassiter dreamed of dark-eyed Dona Esperanza, the young and pretty widow of his compadre, Don Benito.